The Sailcloth Shroud

The Sailcloth Shroud

CHARLES WILLIAMS

NEW YORK: THE VIKING PRESS

The Sailcloth Shroud

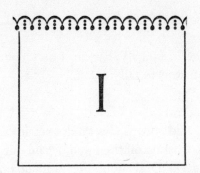

I was up the mainmast of the *Topaz* in a bosun's chair when the police car drove into the yard, around eleven o'clock Saturday morning. The yard doesn't work on Saturdays, so there was no one around except me, and the watchman out at the gate. The car stopped near the end of the pier at which the *Topaz* was moored, and two men got out. I glanced at them without much interest and went on with my work, hand-sanding the mast from which the old varnish had been removed. They were probably looking for some exuberant type off the shrimp boat, I thought. She was the *Leila M.*, the only other craft in the yard at the moment.

They came on out on the pier in the blazing sunlight, however, and halted opposite the mainmast to look up at me. They wore lightweight suits and soft straw hats, and their shirts were wilted with perspiration.

"Your name Rogers?" one of them asked. He was middle-aged, with a square, florid face and expressionless gray eyes. "Stuart Rogers?"

"That's right," I said. "What can I do for you?"

"Police. We want to talk to you."

"Go ahead."

"You come down."

I shrugged, and shoved the sandpaper into a pocket of my dungarees. Casting off the hitch, I paid out the line and dropped on deck. Dust from the sanding operation was plastered to the sweat on my face and torso. I mopped at it with a handkerchief and got a little of it off. I stepped onto the pier, stuck a cigarette in my mouth, and offered the pack to the two men. They shook their heads.

"My name's Willetts," the older one said. "This is my partner, Joe Ramirez."

Ramirez nodded. He was a young man with rather startling blue eyes in a good-looking Latin face. He appraised the *Topaz* with admiration. "Nice-looking schooner you got there."

"Ketch—" I started to say, but let it go. What was the use getting involved in that? "Thanks. What did you want to see me about?"

"You know a man named Keefer?" Willetts asked.

"Sure." I flicked the lighter and grinned. "Has he made the sneezer again?"

Willetts ignored the question. "How well do you know him?"

"About three weeks' worth," I replied. I nodded toward the ketch. "He helped me sail her up from Panama."

"Describe him."

"He's about thirty-eight. Black hair, blue eyes. Five-ten, maybe; a hundred and sixty to a hundred and seventy pounds. Has a chipped tooth in front. And a tattoo on his right arm. Heart, with a girl's name in it. Doreen, Charlene —one of those. Why?"

It was like pouring information into a hole in the ground. I got nothing back, not even a change of expression.

"When was the last time you saw him?"

"Couple of nights ago, I think."

"You think? Don't you know?"

I was beginning to care very little for his attitude, but I kept it to myself. Barking back at policemen is a sucker's game. "I didn't enter it in the log, if that's what you mean," I said. "But, let's see. This is Saturday—so it must have been Thursday night. Around midnight."

The detectives exchanged glances. "You better come along with us," Willetts said.

"What for?"

"Verify an identification, for one thing—"

"Identification?"

"Harbor Patrol fished a stiff out from under Pier Seven this morning. We think it may be your friend Keefer, but we haven't got much to go on."

I stared at him. "You mean he's drowned?"

"No," he said curtly. "Somebody killed him."

"Oh," I said. Beyond the boatyard the surface of the bay burned like molten glass in the sun, unbroken except for the bow wave of a loaded tanker headed seaward from one of the refineries above. Keefer was no prize, God knows, and I hadn't particularly liked him, but— It was hard to sort out.

"Let's go," Willetts said. "You want to change clothes?"

"Yeah." I flipped the cigarette outward into the water and stepped back aboard. The detectives followed me below. They stood watching while I took a change of clothing and a towel from the drawer under one of the bunks in the after cabin. When I started back up the companionway, Willetts asked, "Haven't you got a bathroom on here?"

"No water aboard at the moment," I replied. "I use the yard washroom."

"Oh." They went back on deck and accompanied me up the pier in the muggy Gulf Coast heat. "We'll wait for you in the car," Willetts said. The washroom was in a small building attached to one end of the machine shop, off to the right and beyond the marine ways. I stripped and showered. Could it be Keefer they were talking about? He was a drunk, and could have been rolled, but why killed and thrown in the bay? And by this time he couldn't have had more than a few dollars, anyway. The chances were it wasn't Keefer at all.

I toweled myself and dressed in faded washable slacks, sneakers, and a short-sleeved white shirt. After slipping the watch back on my wrist, I transferred wallet, cigarettes, and lighter, took the dungarees aboard the *Topaz*, and snapped the padlock on the companion hatch.

Ramirez drove. The old watchman looked up curiously from his magazine as we went out the gate. Willetts hitched around on the front seat. "You picked up this guy Keefer in Panama, is that it?"

I lighted a cigarette and nodded. "He'd missed his ship in Cristobal, and wanted a ride back to the States."

"Why didn't he fly back?"

"He was broke."

"What?"

"He didn't have plane fare."

"How much did you pay him?"

"Hundred dollars. Why?"

Willetts made no reply. The car shot across the railroad tracks and into the warehouse and industrial district bordering the waterfront.

"I don't get it," I said. "Wasn't there any identification on this body you found in the bay?"

"No."

"Then what makes you think it might be Keefer?"

"Couple of things," Willetts said shortly. "Was this his home port?"

"I don't think so," I said. "He told me he shipped out of Philadelphia."

"What else you know about him?"

"He's an A.B. His full name is Francis L. Keefer, but he was usually known as Blackie. Apparently something of a live-it-up type. Said he'd been in trouble with the union before, for missing ships. This time he was on an intercoastal freighter, bound for San Pedro. Went ashore in Cristobal, got a heat on, and wound up in jail over in the Panamanian side, in Colón. The ship sailed without him."

"So he asked you for a job?"

"That's right."

"Kind of funny, wasn't it? I mean, merchant seamen don't usually ship out on puddle-jumpers like yours, do they?"

"No, but I don't think you get the picture. He was stranded. Flat broke. He had the clothes he was wearing, and the whisky shakes, and that was about it. I had to advance him twenty dollars to buy some dungarees and gear for the trip."

"And there were just the three of you? You and Keefer, and this other guy, that died at sea? What was his name?"

"Baxter," I said.

"Was he a merchant seaman too?"

"No. He was an office worker of some kind. Accountant, I think—though that's just a guess."

"Hell, didn't he say what he did?"

"He didn't talk much. As a matter of fact, he was twice the seamen Keefer was, but I don't think he'd ever been a pro."

"Did you and Keefer have any trouble?"

"No."

The pale eyes fixed on my face, as expressionless as marbles. "None at all? From the newspaper story, it was a pretty rugged trip."

"It was no picnic," I said.

"You didn't have a fight, or anything?"

"No. Oh, I chewed him out for splitting the mains'l, but you'd hardly call it a fight. He had it coming, and knew it."

The car paused briefly for a traffic light, and turned, weaving through the downtown traffic. "What's this about a sail?"

"It's technical. Just say he goofed, and wrecked it. It was right after Baxter died, and I was jumpy anyway, so I barked at him."

"You haven't kept in touch with him since you got in?"

"No. I haven't seen him since I paid him off, except for that few minutes night before last."

The car slowed, and turned down a ramp into a cavernous basement garage in which several patrol cars and an ambulance were parked. We slid into a numbered stall and got out. Across the garage was an elevator, and to the left of it a dingy corridor. Willetts led the way down the corridor to a doorway on the right.

Inside was a bleak room of concrete and calcimine and unshaded light. On either side were the vaults that were the grisly filing cabinets of a city's unclaimed and anonymous dead, and at the far end a stairway led up to the floor above. Near the stairway were two or three enameled metal tables on casters, and a desk at which sat an old man in a white coat. He got up and came toward us, carrying a clip board.

"Four," Willetts said.

The old man pulled the drawer out on its rollers. The body was covered with a sheet. Ramirez took a corner of it in his hand, and glanced at me. "If you had any breakfast, better hang onto it."

He pulled it back. In spite of myself, I sucked in my breath, the sound just audible in the stillness. He wasn't pretty. I fought the revulsion inside me, and forced myself to look again. It was Blackie, all right; there was little doubt of it, in spite of the wreckage of his face. There was no blood, of course—it had long since been washed away by the water —but the absence of it did nothing to lessen the horror of the beating he had taken before he died.

"Well?" Willetts asked in his flat, unemotional voice. "That Keefer?"

I nodded. "How about the tattoo?"

Ramirez pulled the sheet back farther, exposing the nude body. On one forearm was the blue outline of a valentine heart with the name *Darlene* written slantingly across it in red script. That settled it. I turned away, remembering a heaving deck and wind-hurled rain, and holding Keefer by the front of his sodden shirt while I cursed him. I'm sorry, Blackie. I wish I hadn't.

"There's no doubt of it?" Willetts asked. "That's the guy you brought up from Panama?"

"No doubt at all," I replied. "It's Keefer."

"Okay. Let's go upstairs."

The room was on the third floor, an airless cubicle with one dirty window looking out over the sun-blasted gravel roof of an adjoining building. The only furnishings were some steel lockers, a table scarred with old cigarette burns, and several straight-backed chairs.

Willetts nodded to Ramirez. "Joe, tell the lieutenant we're here."

Ramirez went out. Willetts dropped his hat on the table, took off his coat, and loosened the collar of his shirt. After removing a pack of cigarettes from the coat, he draped it across the back of one of the chairs. "Sit down."

I sat down at the table. The room was stifling, and I could feel sweat beading my face. I wished I could stop seeing Keefer. "Why in the name of God did they beat him that way? Is that what actually killed him?"

Willetts popped a match with his thumbnail, and exhaled

smoke. "He was pistol-whipped. And killed by a blow on the back of his head. But suppose we ask the questions, huh? And don't try to hold out on me, Rogers; we can make you wish you'd never been born."

I felt a quick ruffling of anger, but kept it under control. "Why the hell would I hold out on you? If there's any way I can help, I'll be glad to. What do you want to know?"

"Who you are, to begin with. What you're doing here. And how you happened to be sailing that boat up from Panama."

"I bought her in the Canal Zone," I said. I took out my wallet and flipped identification onto the table—Florida driver's license, FCC license verification card, and memberships in a Miami Beach sportsman's club and the Miami Chamber of Commerce. Willetts made a note of the address. "I own the schooner *Orion*. She berths at the City Yacht Basin in Miami, and makes charter cruises through the Bahamas—"

"So why'd you buy another one?"

"I'm trying to tell you, if you'll give me a chance. Summer's the slow season, from now till the end of October, and the *Orion's* tied up. I heard about this deal on the *Topaz*, through a yacht broker who's a friend of mine. Some oil-rich kids from Oklahoma bought her a couple of months ago and took off for Tahiti without bothering to find out if they could sail a boat across Biscayne Bay. With a little luck, they managed to get as far as the Canal, but they'd had a belly-full of glamour and romance and being seasick twenty-four hours a day, so they left her there and flew back. I was familiar with her, and knew she'd bring twice the asking price back in the States, so I made arrangements with the bank for a loan, hopped the next Pan American flight down there, and looked her over and bought her."

"Why'd you bring her over here, instead of Florida?"

"Better chance of a quick sale. Miami's always flooded with boats."

"And you hired Keefer, and this man Baxter, to help you?"

"That's right. She's a little too much boat for single-handed operation, and sailing alone's just a stunt, anyway. But four days out of Cristobal, Baxter died of a heart attack—"

"I read the story in the paper," Willetts said. He sat down and leaned his forearms on the table. "All right, let's get to Keefer. And what I want to know is where he got all his money."

I looked at him. "Money? He didn't—"

"I know, I know!" Willetts cut me off. "That's what you keep telling me. You picked him up off the beach in Panama with his tail hanging out. He didn't have a nickel, no luggage, and no clothes except the ones he was wearing. And all you paid him was a hundred dollars. Right?"

"Yes."

Willetts gestured with his cigarette. "Well, you better look again. We happen to know that when he came ashore off that boat he had somewhere between three and four thousand dollars."

"Not a chance. We must be talking about two different people."

"Listen, Rogers. When they pulled Keefer out of the bay,

he was wearing a new suit that cost a hundred and seventy-five dollars. For the past four days he's been driving a rented Thunderbird, and living at the Warwick Hotel, which is no skid-row flop, believe me. And he's still the richest stiff in the icebox. They're holding an envelope for him in the Warwick safe with twenty-eight hundred dollars in it. Now you tell me."

II

I sʜᴏᴏᴋ my head in bewilderment. "I don't get it. Are you sure about all this?"

"Of course we're sure. Where you think we first got a lead on the identification? We got a body, with no name. Traffic's got a wrinkled Thunderbird with rental platcs somebody walked off and abandoned after laying a block on a fire hydrant with it, and a complaint sworn out by the Willard Rental Agency. The Willard manager's got a description, and a local address at the Warwick Hotel, and a name. Only this Francis Keefer they're all trying to locate hasn't been in his room since Thursday, and he sounds a lot like the stiff we're trying to identify. He'd been tossing big tips around the Warwick, and told one of the bellhops he'd just sailed up from Panama in a private yacht, so then somebody remembered the story in Wednesday's *Telegram*. So we look you up, among other things, and you give us this song and dance that Keefer was just a merchant seaman, and broke.

Now. Keefer lied to you, or you're trying to con me. And if you are, God help you."

The whole thing was crazy. "Why the hell would I lie about it?" I asked. "And I tell you he was a seaman. Look, weren't his papers in his gear at the hotel?"

"No. Just some new luggage, and new clothes. If he had any papers, they must have been on him when he was killed, and ditched along with the rest of his identification. We know he had a Pennsylvania driver's license. That's being checked out now. But let's get back to the money."

"Well, maybe he had a savings account somewhere. I'll admit it doesn't sound much like Keefer—"

"No. Listen. You docked here Monday afternoon. Tuesday morning you were both tied up in the US marshal's office on that Baxter business. So it was Tuesday afternoon before you paid Keefer off. What time did he finally leave the boat?"

"Three p.m. Maybe a little later."

"Well, there you are. If he sent somewhere for that much money, it'd have to come through a bank. And they were closed by then. But when he checked in at the Warwick, a little after four, *he had the money with him.* In cash."

"It throws me," I said. "I don't know where he could have got it. But I do know he was a seaman. You can verify that with the US marshal's office and the Coast Guard. He had to witness the log entries and sign the affidavits, so they've got a record of his papers."

"We're checking that," Willetts cut in brusquely. "Look —could he have had that money on the boat all the time without you knowing it?"

"Of course."

"How? It's not a very big boat, and you were out there over two weeks."

"Well, naturally I didn't prowl through his personal gear. It could have been in the drawer under his bunk. But I still say he didn't have it. I got to know him pretty well, and I don't think he had any money at all."

"Why?"

"Two reasons, at least. If he hadn't been on his uppers, he wouldn't even have considered working his way back to the States on a forty-foot ketch. Keefer was no small-boat man. He knew nothing about sail, and cared less. His idea of going to sea was eighteen knots, fresh-water showers, and overtime. So if he'd had any money he'd have bought a plane ticket—except that he'd have gone on another binge and spent it. When I met him, he didn't have the price of a drink. And he needed one."

"All right. So he left Panama flat broke, and got here with four thousand dollars. I can see I'm in the wrong racket. How much money did you have aboard?"

"About six hundred."

"Then he must have clouted it from Baxter."

I shook my head. "When Baxter died, I made an inventory of his personal effects, and entered it in the log. He had about a hundred and seventy dollars in his wallet. The marshal's office has it, along with the rest of his gear, to be turned over to his next of kin."

"Maybe Keefer beat you to it."

"Baxter couldn't have had that kind of money; it's out of the question. He was about as schooner-rigged as Keefer."

"Schooner-rigged?"

"Short of clothes and luggage. He didn't talk about it, any more than he did anything else, but you could see he was down on his luck. And he was sailing up because he wanted to save the plane fare. But why is the money so important, even if we don't know where Keefer got it? What's it got to do with his being butchered and dumped in the bay?"

Before Willetts could reply, Ramirez appeared in the doorway. He motioned, and Willetts got up and went out. I could hear the murmur of their voices in the hall. I walked over to the window. A fly was buzzing with futile monotony against one of the dirty panes, and heat shimmered above the gravel of the roof next door. They seemed to know what they were talking about, so it must be true. And if you knew Keefer, it was in character—the big splash, the free-wheeling binge, even the wrecked Thunderbird—a thirty-eight-year-old adolescent with an unexpected fortune. But where had he got it? That was as baffling as the senseless brutality with which he'd been killed.

The two detectives came back and motioned for me to sit down. "All right," Willetts said. "You saw him Thursday night. Where was this, and when?"

"Waterfront beer joint called the Domino," I said. "It's not far from the boatyard, up a couple of blocks and across the tracks. I think the time was around eleven-thirty. I'd been uptown to a movie, and was coming back to the yard. I stopped in for a beer before I went aboard. Keefer was there, with some girl he'd picked up."

"Was there anybody with him besides the girl?"

"No."

"Tell us just what happened."

"The place was fairly crowded, but I found a stool at the bar. Just as I got my beer I looked around, and saw Keefer and the girl in a booth behind me. I walked over and spoke to him. He was pretty drunk, and the girl was about half-crocked herself, and they were arguing."

"What was her name?"

"He didn't introduce us. I just stayed for a moment and went back to the bar."

"Describe her."

"Brassy type. Thin blonde, in her early twenties. Dangly earrings, plucked eyebrows, too much mascara. I think she said she was a cashier in a restaurant. The bartender seemed to know her."

"Did they leave first, or did you?"

"She left, alone. About ten minutes later. I don't know what they were fighting about, but all of a sudden she got up, bawled him out, and left. Keefer came over to the bar then. He seemed to be relieved to get rid of her. We talked for a while. I asked him if he'd registered at the hiring hall for a job yet, and he said he had but shipping was slow. He wanted to know if I'd had any offers for the *Topaz,* and when I thought the yard would be finished with her."

"Was he flashing money around?"

"Not unless it was before I got there. While we were sitting at the bar he ordered a round of drinks, but I wouldn't let him pay, thinking he was about broke. When we finished them, he wanted to order more, but he'd had way too much. I tried to get him to eat something, but didn't have much luck. This place is a sort of longshoremen's hangout, and in the rear of it there's a small lunch counter. I took him back and ordered him a hamburger and a cup of black coffee. He did drink the coffee—"

"Hold it a minute," Willetts broke in. "Did he eat any of the hamburger at all?"

"About two bites. Why?"

They looked at each other, ignoring me. Ramirez turned to go out, but Willetts shook his head. "Wait a minute, Joe. Let's get the rest of this story first, and you can ask the lieutenant for some help in checking it out."

He turned back to me. "Did you and Keefer leave the bar together?"

"No. He left first. Right after he drank the coffee. He was weaving pretty badly, and I was afraid he'd pass out somewhere, so I tried to get him to let me call a cab to take him back to wherever he was staying, but he didn't want one. When I insisted, he started to get nasty. Said he didn't need any frilling nurse; he was holding his liquor when I was in diapers. He staggered on out. I finished my beer, and left about ten minutes later. I didn't see him anywhere on the street."

"Did anybody follow him out?"

"No-o. Not that I noticed."

"And that would have been just a little before twelve?"

I thought about it. "Yes. As a matter of fact, the four-to-midnight watchman had just been relieved when I came in the gate at the boatyard, and was still there, talking to the other one."

"And they saw you, I suppose?"

"Sure. They checked me in."

"Did you go out again that night?"

I shook my head. "Not till about six-thirty the next morning, for breakfast."

Willetts turned to Ramirez. "Okay, Joe." The latter went out.

"There's no way in and out of the yard except past the watchman?" Willetts asked.

"I don't think so," I replied.

Ramirez came back, carrying a sheet of paper. He handed it to Willetts. "That checks, all right."

Willetts glanced at it thoughtfully and nodded. He spoke to me. "That boat locked?"

"Yes," I said. "Why?"

"Give Joe the key. We want to look it over."

I stared at him coldly. "What for?"

"This is a murder investigation, friend. But if you insist, we'll get a warrant. And lock you up till we finish checking your story. Do it easy, do it hard—it's up to you."

I shrugged, and handed over the key. Ramirez nodded pleasantly, nullifying some of the harshness of Willetts' manner. He went out. Willetts studied the paper again, drumming his fingers on the table. Then he refolded it. "Your story seems to tie in okay with this."

"What's that?" I asked.

"The autopsy report. I mean those two bites of hamburger he ate. It's always hard to place the time of death this long afterward, especially if the body's been in the water, so about all they had to go on was what was in his stomach. And that's no help if you can't find out when he ate last. But if that counterman at the Domino backs you up, we can peg it pretty well. Keefer was killed sometime between two and three a.m."

"It couldn't have been much later than that," I said. "They couldn't dump him off a pier in broad daylight, and it's dawn before five o'clock."

"There's no telling where he was thrown in," Willetts said. "It was around seven-thirty this morning when they found him, so he'd have been in the water over twenty-four hours."

I nodded. "With four changes of tide. As a matter of fact, you were probably lucky he came to the surface this soon."

"Propellers, the Harbor Patrol said. Some tugs were docking a ship at Pier Seven and washed him to the surface and somebody saw him and called them."

"Where did they find the car?"

"The three-hundred block on Armory. That's a good mile from the waterfront, and about the same distance from the area that beer joint's in. A patrol car spotted it at one-twenty-five Thursday morning. That'd be about an hour and a half after he left the joint, but there wasn't anybody in sight, so they don't know what time it happened. Could have been within a few minutes after you saw him. The car'd jumped the curb, sideswiped a fireplug, pulled back into the street again, and gone on another fifty yards before it jammed over against the curb once more and stopped. Might have been just a drunken accident, but I don't quite buy it. I think he was forced to the curb by another car."

"Teen-age hoodlums, maybe?"

Willetts shook his head. "Not that time of morning. Any ducktails blasting around in hot-rods after midnight get a fast shuffle around here. And there wasn't a mark on his hands; he didn't hit anybody. That sounds like professional muscle to me."

"But why would they kill him?"

"You tell me." Willetts stood up and reached for his hat. "Let's go in the office. Lieutenant Boyd wants to see you after a while."

We went down the corridor to a doorway at the far end. Inside was a long room containing several desks and a battery of steel filing cabinets. The floor was of battered brown linoleum held down by strips of brass. Most of the rear wall was taken up with a duty roster and two bulletin boards festooned with typewritten notices and circulars. A pair of half-open windows on the right looked out over the street. At the far end of the room a frosted glass door apparently led to an inner office. One man in shirtsleeves was typing a report at a desk; he glanced up incuriously and went on with his work. Traffic noise filtered up from the street to mingle with the lifeless air and its stale smells of old dust and cigar smoke and sweaty authority accumulated over the years and a thousand past investigations. Willetts nodded to a chair before one of the vacant desks. I sat down, wondering impatiently how much longer it was going to take. I had plenty to do aboard the *Topaz*. Then I thought guiltily of Keefer's savagely mutilated face down there under the sheet. *You're* griping about your troubles?

Willetts lowered his bulk into a chair behind the desk, took some papers from a drawer, and studied them for a moment. "Did Keefer and Baxter know each other?" he asked. "I mean, before they shipped out with you?"

"No," I said.

"You sure of that?"

"I introduced them. So far as I know, they'd never seen each other before."

"Which one did you hire first?"

"Keefer. I didn't even meet Baxter until the night before we sailed. But what's that got to do with Keefer's being killed?"

"I don't know." Willetts returned to his study of the papers on his desk. Somewhere in the city a whistle sounded. It was noon. I lighted another cigarette, and resigned myself to waiting. Two detectives came in with a young girl who was crying. I could hear them questioning her at the other end of the room.

Willetts shoved the papers aside and leaned back in his chair. "I still don't get this deal you couldn't make it ashore with Baxter's body. You were only four days out of the Canal."

I sighed. Here was another Monday-morning quarterback. It wasn't enough to have the Coast Guard looking down your throat; you had to be second-guessed by jokers who wouldn't know a starboard tack from a reef point. It was simple, actually; all you had to be was a navigator, seaman, cardiologist, sailmaker, embalmer, and a magician's mate first class who could pull a breeze out of his hat. Then I realized, for perhaps the twentieth time, that I was being too defensive and antagonistic about it. The memory rankled because I was constitutionally unable to bear the sensation of helplessness. And I had been helpless.

"The whole thing's a matter of record," I said wearily.

"There was a hearing—" I broke off as the phone rang on an adjoining desk. Willetts reached for it.

"Homicide, Willetts. . . . Yeah. . . . Nothing at all? . . . Yeah. . . . Yeah. . . ." The conversation went on for two or three minutes. Then Willetts said, "Okay, Joe. You might as well come on in."

He replaced the instrument, and swung back to me. "Before I forget it, the yard watchman's got your key. Let's go in and see Lieutenant Boyd."

The room beyond the frosted glass door was smaller, and contained a single desk. The shirtsleeved man behind it was in his middle thirties, with massive shoulders, an air of tough assurance, and probing gray eyes that were neither friendly nor unfriendly.

"This is Rogers," Willetts said.

Boyd stood up and held out his hand. "I've read about you," he said briefly.

We sat down. Boyd lighted a cigarette and spoke to Willetts. "You come up with anything yet?"

"Positive identification by Rogers and the manager of the car-rental place. Also that bellhop from the Warwick. So Keefer's all one man. But nobody's got any idea where he found all that money. Rogers swears he couldn't have had it when he left Panama." He went on, repeating all I'd told him.

When he had finished, Boyd asked, "How does his story check out?"

"Seems to be okay. We haven't located the girl yet, but the night bartender in that joint knows her, and remembers the three of 'em. He's certain Keefer left there about the time Rogers gave us; says Keefer got pretty foul-mouthed about not wanting the taxi Rogers was going to call, so he told him to shut up or get out. The watchman at the boat-yard says Rogers was back there at five minutes past twelve, and didn't go out again. That piece of hamburger jibes with the autopsy report, and puts the time he was killed between two and three in the morning."

Boyd nodded. "And you think Keefer had the Thunderbird parked outside the joint then?"

"Looks that way," Willetts conceded.

"It would make sense, so Rogers must be leveling about the money. Keefer didn't want him to see the car and start getting curious. Anything on the boat?"

"No. Joe says it's clean. No gun, no money, nothing. Doesn't prove anything, necessarily."

"No. But we've got nothing to hold Rogers for."

"How about till we can check him out with Miami? And get a report back from the Bureau on Keefer's prints?"

"No," Boyd said crisply.

Willetts savagely stubbed out his cigarette. "But, damn it, Jim, something stinks in this whole deal—"

"Save it! You can't book a smell."

"Take a look at it!" Willetts protested. "Three men leave Panama in a boat with about eight hundred dollars between 'em. One disappears in the middle of the ocean, and another one comes ashore with four thousand dollars, and four days later *he's* dead—"

"Hold it!" I said. "If you're accusing me of something, let's hear what it is. Nobody's 'disappeared,' as you call it.

Baxter died of a heart attack. There was a hearing, with a doctor present, and it's been settled—"

"On your evidence. And one witness, who's just been murdered."

"Cut it out!" the lieutenant barked. He jerked an impatient hand at Willetts. "For Christ's sake, we've got no jurisdiction in the Caribbean Sea. Baxter's death was investigated by the proper authorities, and if they're satisfied, I am. And when I am, *you* are. Now get somebody to run Rogers back to his boat. If we need him again, we can pick him up."

I stood up. "Thanks," I said. "I'll be around for another week, at least. Maybe two."

"Right," Boyd said. The telephone rang on his desk, and he cut short the gesture of dismissal to reach for it. We went out, and started across the outer office. Just before we reached the corridor, we were halted by the lieutenant's voice behind us. "Wait a minute! Hold everything!"

We turned. Boyd had his head out the door of his office. "Bring Rogers back here a minute." We went back. Boyd was on the telephone. "Yeah. . . . He's still here. . . . In the office. . . . Right."

He replaced the instrument, and nodded to me. "You might as well park it again. That was the FBI."

I looked at him, puzzled. "What do they want?"

"You mean they ever tell anybody? They just said to hold you till they could get a man over here."

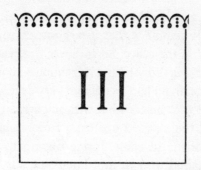

III

At least, I thought morosely as we stepped from the elevator, the Federal Building was air-conditioned. If you were going to spend the rest of your life being questioned about Keefer by all the law-enforcement agencies in the country, it helped a little if you were comfortable. Not that I had anything against heat as such; I liked hot countries, provided they were far enough away from civilization to do away with the wearing of shirts that did nothing but stick to you like some sort of soggy film. The whole day was shot to hell now, but this was an improvement over the police station.

I glanced sidewise in grudging admiration at Special Agent Soames—cool, efficient, and faultlessly pressed. Sweat would never be any problem to this guy; if it bothered him he'd turn it off. In the ten minutes since I'd met him in Lieutenant Boyd's office, I'd learned exactly nothing about why they wanted to talk to me. I'd asked, when we were out

on the street, and had been issued a friendly smile and one
politely affable assurance that it was merely routine. We'd
discuss it over in the office. Soames was thirty-ish and crew-
cut, but anything boyish and ingenuous about him was
strictly superficial; he had a cool and very deadly eye.

We went down the corridor, with my crepe soles squeak-
ing on waxed tile. Soames opened a frosted glass door and
stood aside for me to enter. Inside was a small anteroom.
A trim gray-haired woman in a linen suit was typing ener-
getically at a desk that held a telephone and a switchbox
for routing calls. Behind her was the closed door to an inner
office, and to the left I could see down a hallway past a
number of other doors. Soames looked at his watch and
wrote something in the book that was on a small desk near
the door. Then he nodded politely, and said, "This way,
please."

I followed him down the hallway to the last door. The
office inside was small, spotlessly neat, and cool, with light
green walls, marbled gray linoleum, and one window, across
which were tilted the white slats of a venetian blind. There
was a single desk, with a swivel chair in back of it. An armchair stood before it, near one corner, facing the light from
the window. Soames nodded toward it, and held out cigarettes. "Sit down, please. I'll be right back."

I fired up the cigarette. As I dropped the lighter back
in my pocket, I said curiously, "I don't get this. Why is the
FBI interested in Keefer?"

"Keefer?" Soames had started out; he paused in the doorway. "Oh, that's a local police matter."

I stared blankly after him. If they weren't interested in

Keefer, what *did* they want to know? Soames returned in a moment carrying a Manila folder. He sat down and began emptying it of its contents: the log I had kept of the trip, the signed and notarized statement regarding Baxter's death, and the inventory of his personal effects.

He glanced up briefly. "I suppose you're familiar with all this?"

"Yes, of course," I said. "But how'd it get over here? And just what is it you want?"

"We're interested in Wendell Baxter." Soames slid the notarized statement out of the pile, and studied it thoughtfully. "I haven't had much chance to digest this, or your log, so I'd like to check the facts with you just briefly, if you don't mind."

"Not at all," I replied. "But I thought the whole thing was closed. The marshal's office—"

"Oh, yes," Soames assured me. "It's just that they've run into a little difficulty in locating Baxter's next of kin, and they've asked us to help."

"I see."

He went on crisply. "You're owner and captain of the forty-foot ketch *Topaz*, which you bought in Cristobal, Panama Canal Zone, on May twenty-seven of this year, through Joseph Hillyer, Miami yacht broker who represented the sellers. That's correct?"

"Right."

"You sailed from Cristobal on June one, at ten-twenty a.m., bound for this port, accompanied by two other men you engaged as deckhands for the trip. One was Francis L. Keefer, a merchant seaman, possessing valid A.B. and Lifeboat certificates as per indicated numbers, American national, born in Buffalo, New York, September twelve, nineteen-twenty. The other was Wendell Baxter, occupation or profession unspecified but believed to be of a clerical nature, not possessed of seaman's papers of any kind but obviously familiar with the sea and well versed in the handling of small sailing craft such as yachts, home address San Francisco, California. Four days out of Cristobal, on June five, Baxter collapsed on deck at approximately three-thirty p.m. while trimming a jib sheet, and died about twenty minutes later. There was nothing you could do to help him, of course. You could find no medicine in his suitcase, the boat's medicine chest contained nothing but the usual first-aid supplies, and you were several hundred miles from the nearest doctor."

"That's right," I said. "If I never feel that helpless again, it'll be all right with me."

Soames nodded. "Your position at the time was 16.10 North, 81.40 West, some four hundred miles from the Canal, and approximately a hundred miles off the coast of Honduras. It was obvious you were at least another six days from the nearest Stateside port, so you put about immediately to return to the Canal Zone with his body, but in three days you saw you were never going to get there in time. That's essentially it?"

"In three days we made eighty-five miles," I said. "And the temperature down there in the cabin where his body was ran around ninety degrees."

"You couldn't have gone into some port in Honduras?"

I gestured impatiently. "This has all been threshed out

with the Coast Guard. I could have tried for some port on the mainland of Honduras or Nicaragua, or gone on to Georgetown, Grand Cayman, which was less than two hundred miles to the north of us—except that I wasn't cleared for any of those places. Baxter was already dead, so it's doubtful the port authorities would have considered it a legitimate emergency. And just to come plowing in unauthorized, with no bill of health or anything, carrying the body of a man who'd died at sea of some unspecified ailment—we'd have been slapped in quarantine and tied up in red tape till we had beards down to our knees. Besides being fined. The only thing to do was go back."

"And you had nothing but bad luck, right from the beginning?"

"Look," I said hotly, "we tried. We tried till we couldn't stand it any longer. Believe me, I didn't want the responsibility of burying him at sea. In the first place, it wasn't going to be pleasant facing his family. And if we couldn't bring the body ashore for an autopsy, there'd have to be a hearing of some kind to find out what he died of. There's nothing new about burial at sea, of course, especially in the old days when ships were a lot slower than they are now, but a merchant or naval vessel with thirty to several hundred people aboard is—well, a form of community itself, with somebody in authority and dozens of witnesses. Three men alone in a small boat would be something else. When only two come back, you're going to have to have a little better explanation than just saying Bill dropped dead and we threw him overboard. That's the reason for all that detailed report on the symptoms of the attack. I wrote

it out as soon as I saw we were probably going to have to
do it."

Soames nodded. "It's quite thorough. Apparently the
doctor who reviewed it had no difficulty in diagnosing the
seizure as definitely some form of heart attack, and probably a coronary thrombosis. I wonder if you'd fill me in
just briefly on what happened after you started back?"

"To begin with," I said, "we tore the mains'l all to hell.
The weather had turned unsettled that morning, even before
Baxter had the attack. Just before dusk I could see a squall
making up to the eastward. It looked a little dirty, but I
didn't want to shorten down any more than we had to,
considering the circumstances. So we left everything on, and
just turned in a couple of reefs in the main and mizzen. Or
started to. We were finishing the main when it began to
kick up a little and the rain hit us. I ran back to the wheel
to keep her into the wind, while Keefer tied in the last few
points and started to raise sail again. I suppose it's my fault
for not checking, but I'd glanced off toward the squall line
and when I looked back at the mains'l it was too late. He
had the halyard taut and was throwing it on the winch.
I yelled for him to slack off, but with all the rain he didn't
hear me. What had happened was that he'd mixed up a pair
of reef points—tied one from the second row to another on
the opposite side in the third set. That pulls the sail out
of shape and puts all the strain in one place. It was just
a miracle it hadn't let go already. I screamed at him again,
and he finally heard me this time and looked around, but
all he did was shake his head that he couldn't understand
what I was saying. Just as I jumped from behind the wheel

and started to run forward he slipped the handle into the winch and took a turn, and that was the ball game. It split all the way across.

"We didn't have another one aboard. The previous owners had pretty well butched up the sail inventory on the way down to the Canal—blew out a mains'l and lost the genoa overboard. I managed to patch up this one after a fashion, using material out of an old stays'l, but it took two days. Maybe it wouldn't have made much difference, anyway, because the weather went completely sour—dead calm about half the time, with occasional light airs that hauled all around the compass. But with just that handkerchief of a mizzen, and stays'l and working jib, we might as well have been trying to row her to the Canal. We ran on the auxiliary till we used up all the gasoline aboard, and then when there was no wind we just drifted. Keefer kept moaning and griping for us to get rid of him; said he couldn't sleep in the cabin with a dead man. And neither of us could face the thought of trying to prepare any food with him lying there just forward of the galley. We finally moved out on deck altogether.

"By Sunday morning—June eighth—I knew it had to be done. I sewed him in what was left of the old stays'l, with the sounding lead at his feet. It was probably an all-time low in funerals. I couldn't think of more than a half dozen words of the sea-burial service, and there was no Bible aboard. We did shave and put on shirts, and that was about it. We buried him at one p.m. The position's in the log, and I think it's fairly accurate. The weather improved that night, and we came on here and arrived on the sixteenth. Along with the report, I turned his personal belongings over to the marshal's office. But I don't understand why they couldn't locate some of his family; his address is right there—1426 Roland Avenue, San Francisco."

"Unfortunately," Soames replied, "there is no Roland Avenue in San Francisco."

"Oh," I said.

"So we hoped you might be able to help us."

I frowned, feeling vaguely uneasy. For some reason I was standing at the rail again on that day of oily calm and blistering tropic sun, watching the body in its Orlon shroud as it sank beneath the surface and began its long slide into the abyss. "That's just great," I said. "I don't know anything about him either."

"In four days, he must have told you *something* about himself."

"You could repeat it all in forty seconds. He told me he was an American citizen. His home was in California. He'd come down to the Canal Zone on some job that had folded up after a couple of months, and he'd like to save the plane fare back to the States by sailing up with me."

"He didn't mention the name of any firm, or government agency?"

"Not a word. I gathered it was a clerical or executive job of some kind, because he had the appearance. And his hands were soft."

"He never said anything about a wife? Children? Brothers?"

"Nothing."

"Did he say anything at all during the heart attack?"

"No. He seemed to be trying to, but he couldn't get his breath. And the pain was pretty terrible until he finally lost consciousness."

"I see." Soames' blue eyes were thoughtful. "Would you describe him?"

"I'd say he was around fifty. About my height, six-one. But very slender; I doubt he weighed over a hundred and seventy. Brown eyes, short brown hair with a good deal of gray in it, especially around the temples, but not thinning or receding to any extent. Thin face, rather high forehead, good nose and bone structure, very quiet, and soft-spoken— when he said anything at all. In a movie, you'd cast him as a doctor or lawyer or the head of the English department. That's the thing, you see; he wasn't hard-nosed or rude about not talking about himself; he was just reserved. He minded his own business, and seemed to expect you to mind yours. And since he was apparently down on his luck, it seemed a little on the tasteless side to go prying into matters he didn't want to talk about."

"What about his speech?"

"Well, the outstanding thing about it was that there was damned little of it. But he was obviously well educated. And if there was any trace of a regional accent, I didn't hear it."

"Was there anything foreign about it at all? I don't mean low comedy or vaudeville, but any hesitancy, or awkwardness of phrasing?"

"No," I said. "It was American."

"I see." Soames tapped meditatively on the desk with the eraser end of a pencil. "Now, you say he was an experienced sailor. But he had no papers, and you don't think he'd ever been a merchant seaman, so you must have wondered about it. Could you make any guess as to where he'd picked up this knowledge of the sea?"

"Yes. I think definitely he'd owned and sailed boats of his own, probably boats in the offshore cruising and ocean-racing class. Actually, a merchant seaman wouldn't have known a lot of the things Baxter did, unless he was over seventy and had been to sea under sail. Keefer was a good example. He was a qualified A.B.; he knew routine seamanship, and how to splice and handle line, and if you gave him a compass course he could steer it. But if you were going to windward and couldn't quite lay the course, half the time he'd be lying dead in the water and wouldn't know it. He had no feel. Baxter did. He was one of the best wind-ship helmsmen I've ever run into. Besides native talent, that takes a hell of a lot of experience you don't pick up on farms or by steering power boats or steamships."

"Did he know celestial navigation?"

"Yes," I said. "It's a funny thing, but I think he did. I mean, he never mentioned it, or asked if he could take a sight and work it out for practice, but somehow I got a hunch just from the way he watched me that he knew as much about it as I did. Or maybe more. I'm no whiz; there's not much occasion to use it in the Bahamas."

"Did he ever use a term that might indicate he could have been an ex-Navy officer? Service slang of any kind?"

"No-o. Not that I can recall at the moment. But now you've mentioned it, nearly everything about him would fit. And I'm pretty sure they teach midshipmen to sail at the Academy."

"Yes. I think so."

"He didn't have a class ring, though. No rings of any kind."

"You didn't have a camera aboard, I take it?"

"No," I said.

"That's too bad; a snapshot would have been a great help. What about fingerprints? Can you think of any place aboard we might raise a few? I realize it's been sixteen days—"

"No. I doubt there'd be a chance. She's been in the yard for the past four, and everything's been washed down."

"I see." Soames stood up. "Well, we'll just have to try to locate somebody in the Zone who knew him. Thank you for coming in, Mr. Rogers. We may be in touch with you later, and I'd appreciate it if you would think back over those four days when you have time, and make a note of anything else you recall. You're living aboard, aren't you?"

"Yes."

"Sometimes association helps. You might be reminded of some chance remark he let fall, the name of a city, or yacht club, or something like that. Call us if you think of anything that could help."

"Sure, I'll be glad to," I said. "I don't understand, though, why he would give me a fake address. Do you suppose the name was phony too?"

Soames' expression was polite, but it indicated the conversation was over. "We really have no reason to think so, that I can see."

I walked over and caught a cab in front of the Warwick Hotel. During the ten-minute ride across the city to the eastern end of the waterfront and Harley's boatyard, I tried to make some sense out of the whole affair. Maybe Willetts was right, after all; Keefer could have stolen that money from Baxter's suitcase. If you assumed Baxter had lied about where he was from, he could have been lying about everything. And he'd never actually said he didn't have any money; he'd merely implied it. That was the hell of it; he'd never actually said anything. He became more mysterious every time you looked at him, and when you tried to get hold of something concrete he was as insubstantial as mist.

But what about Keefer? Even if you could bring yourself to accept the premise that he was low enough to steal from a dead man—which was a little hard to swallow— how could he have been that stupid? Maybe he was no mental giant, but still it must have occurred to him that if Baxter was carrying that much money *somebody* must know about it, some friend or relative, and when the money turned up missing there'd be an investigation and charges of theft. Then a disquieting thought occurred to me. So far, nobody had claimed the money. What did you make of that? Had Keefer known, before he took it? But how could he? Then I shrugged, and gave up. Hell, there wasn't even any proof that Keefer had stolen anything.

The taxi bumped across the tracks. I got out at the boatyard entrance and paid off the driver. This end of the waterfront was quiet on Saturday afternoon. To the right was another small shipyard that was closed now, and a half mile beyond that the city yacht basin, and Quarantine, and then the long jetties running out into the open Gulf. To the left were the packing sheds and piers where the shrimp boats clustered in a jungle of masts and suspended nets. These gave way in the next block to the first of the steamship terminals, the big concrete piers and slips that extended along the principal waterfront of the port.

The old watchman swung back the gate. "Here's your key," he said. "They had me come with 'em while they searched the boat. Didn't bother anything."

"Thanks," I said.

"Didn't say what they was looking for," he went on tentatively.

"They didn't tell me either," I said. I went aboard the *Topaz* and changed clothes in the stifling cabin. Nothing was disturbed, as far as I could see. It was only three p.m.; maybe I could still get some work done. I loaded the pockets of my dungarees with sandpaper, went back up the mainmast, and resumed where I'd left off sanding, just below the spreaders. I sat in the bosun's chair, legs gripping the mast to hold myself in against it while I smoothed the surface of the spar with long strokes of the abrasive. For the moment I forgot Keefer, and Baxter, and the whole puzzling mess. This was more like it. If you couldn't be at sea, the next best thing was working about a boat, maintaining her, dressing her until she sparkled, and tuning her until she was like something alive. It seemed almost a shame to offer her for sale, the way she was shaping up.

Money didn't mean much, except as it could be used for the maintenance and improvement of the *Orion*.

I looked forward and aft below me. Another three or four days should do it. She'd already been hauled, scraped, and painted with anti-fouling. Her topsides were a glistening white. The spars and other brightwork had been taken down to the wood, and when I finished sanding this one and the mizzen I could put on the first coat of varnish. Overhaul the tracks and slides, replace the lines in the outhauls, reeve new main and mizzen halyards, replace that frayed head-stay with a piece of stainless steel, give the deck a coat of gray nonskid, and that would about do it. The new mains'l should be here by Tuesday, and the yard ought to have the refrigerator overhauled and back aboard by then. Maybe I'd better jack them up about it again on Monday morning.

Probably start the newspaper ad next Wednesday, I thought. She shouldn't be around long at $15,000, not the way she was designed and built. If I still hadn't sold her in ten days, I'd turn her over to a yacht broker at an asking price of twenty, and go back to Miami. The new mains'l had hurt, and I hadn't counted on having to rebuild the refrigerator, but still I'd be home for less than nine thousand.

Six thousand profit wouldn't be bad for less than two months' work and a little calculated risk. It would mean new batteries and new generator for the *Orion*. A leather lounge and teak table in the saloon. . . . I was down on deck now. I stowed the bosun's chair and began sanding the boom.

"Mr. Rogers!"

I glanced up. It was the watchman, calling to me from

the end of the pier, and I noted with surprise it was the four-to-midnight man, Otto Johns. I'd been oblivious of the passage of time.

"Telephone," he called. "Long distance from New York."

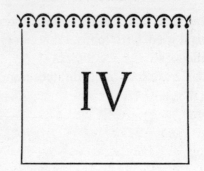

IV

New York? Must be a mistake, I thought as I went up the pier. I didn't know anybody there who would be trying to phone me. The watchman's shack was just inside the gate, with a door and a wide window facing the driveway. Johns set the instrument on the window counter. "Here you go."

I picked it up. "Hello. Rogers speaking."

It was a woman's voice. "Is this the Mr. Stuart Rogers who owns the yacht *Topaz?*"

"That's right."

"Good." There was evident relief in her voice. Then she went on softly, "Mr. Rogers, I'm worried. I haven't heard from him yet."

"From whom?" I asked blankly.

"Oh," she replied. "I *am* sorry. It's just that I'm so upset. This is Paula Stafford."

It was evident from the way she said it the name was

supposed to explain everything. "I don't understand," I said. "What is it you want?"

"He *did* tell you about me, didn't he?"

I sighed. "Miss Stafford—or Mrs. Stafford—I don't know what you're talking about. *Who* told me about you?"

"You're being unnecessarily cautious, Mr. Rogers. I assure you I'm Paula Stafford. It must have been at least two weeks now, and I still have no word from him. I don't like it at all. Do you think something could have gone wrong?"

"Let's go back and start over," I suggested. "My name is Stuart Rogers, age thirty-two, male, single, charter yacht captain—"

"*Will you please—*" she snapped. Then she paused, apparently restraining herself, and went on more calmly. "All right, perhaps you're right not to take chances without some proof. Fortunately, I've already made plane reservations. I'll arrive at two-twenty a.m., and will be at the Warwick Hotel. Will you please meet me there as soon as I check in? It's vitally important." She hung up.

I shrugged, replaced the instrument, and lighted a cigarette. There was a weird one.

"Some nut?" Johns asked. He was a gaunt, white-haired man with ice-blue eyes. He leaned on the window shelf and began stoking a caked and smelly pipe. "I got a son-in-law that's a cop, and he says you get your name in the paper you're pestered with all kindsa screwballs."

"Probably a drunk," I replied.

"Too bad about that Keefer fella," Johns went on. "Did I tell you he was here lookin' for you the other night?"

I glanced up quickly. "He was? When was this?"

"Hmmm. Same night they say he was killed. That'd be Thursday. I reckon I must have forgot to tell you because when you come in Ralph'd just relieved me and we was shootin' the breeze."

"What time was he here?"

"About seven, seven-thirty. Wasn't long after you went out."

I frowned. It was odd that Blackie hadn't mentioned it when I ran into him at the Domino. "You're sure it was Keefer?"

"That's the name he said. Dark-haired kind of fella. Said he was the one that sailed up from Panama with you. I told him you'd gone uptown to a movie and wouldn't be back till around eleven."

"Was he in a car?" I asked. "And was there a girl with him?"

Johns shook his head. "He was by hisself. And I didn't see no car; far as I know he was afoot. I reckon he'd had a couple snorts, because he got pretty hot under the collar when I wouldn't let him go aboard the boat. He told me again about bein' a friend of yours and comin' up from Panama on it, and I said it didn't make no difference to me if he'd helped you sail it here from Omaha, Nebraska. Long as he wasn't in the crew no more he wasn't goin' aboard without you was with him."

"What did he want?" I asked. "Did he say?"

"Said he forgot his razor when he was paid off. I told him he'd have to see you about that. He left, and didn't come back."

"Oh," I said. "The companion hatch was locked; he couldn't have got aboard anyway. He should have known that."

I went back aboard the *Topaz*. It was after six now; I might as well knock off for the day. I walked over to the washroom, showered, shaved, and dressed in clean slacks and a fresh sport shirt. Back in the cabin, as I was putting away my shaving gear, I thought of Keefer. Odd, with all that money he had, that he would come clear back out here just to pick up the cheap shaving kit he'd bought in Panama. I paused. Now that I thought about it, I hadn't even seen it since Keefer had left. Was it just an excuse to get aboard? Maybe the man *was* a thief. I pulled open the drawer under the bunk Keefer had occupied. There was no razor in it. Why, the dirty . . . Well, don't go off halfcocked, I thought; make sure it's not aboard. I stepped into the head and pulled open the tiny medicine cabinet above the basin. There it was, the styrene case containing a safety razor and a pack of blades. My apologies, Blackie.

I went up the companion ladder. The deck now lay in the lengthening shadows of the buildings ashore, and with a slight breeze blowing up bay from the Gulf it was a little cooler. I sat down in the cockpit, took out a cigarette, and then paused just as I started to flip the lighter.

Paula.

Paula Stafford.

Was there something familiar about the name? Hadn't I heard it before, somewhere? Oh, it was probably just imagination. I dropped the lighter back in my pocket, and inhaled deeply of the smoke, but the nagging idea per-

sisted. Maybe Keefer had mentioned her sometime during
the trip. Or Baxter.

Baxter . . . For some reason I was conscious again of
that strange sensation of unease I had felt there in the
office of the FBI. Merely by turning my head I could look
along the port side of the deck, between mizzen and main,
where I had stood that day with head bared to the brazen
heat of the sun and watched the body as it faded slowly
and disappeared, falling silently into the depths and the
crushing pressures and eternal darkness two miles below.
It was the awful finality of it—the fact that if the FBI
couldn't find out something about him, pick up his trail
somewhere, they might never know who he was. There'd
never be a second chance. No fingerprints, no photograph,
no possibility of a better description, nothing. He was gone,
forever, without leaving a trace. Was that it? Was it going to
bother me the rest of my life—the fact that I had failed to
bring the body ashore where it might have been identified?

Oh, hell, I thought angrily, you're just being morbid. You
did everything humanly possible. Except remove the stomach; that would have helped, but you chickened out. So you
did like the man; that's no excuse. It's done. But it wouldn't
have changed anything in the long run. You were still three
hundred miles from the Canal. And in that heat, trying to
stretch it any longer would have been more than just un-
pleasant; it could have become dangerous. Burial was a
practical necessity long before it became a ritual.

But there must be some clue. We'd been together for
four days, and in that length of time even a man as un-
communicative as Baxter would have said *something* that

would provide a lead as to where he was from. Think back. What was it Soames had said about association? Right here within this span of forty feet was where it had all taken place. Start at the beginning, with the first time you ever saw Baxter, and go over every minute.

I stopped. Just why was it necessary? Or rather, why did I feel it was? Why this subconscious fear that they weren't going to find anybody in Panama who knew Baxter? The man said he'd worked there. If he had, the FBI would run him down in a day. Was it merely because the San Francisco address had proved a dead end? No, there must be more. . . .

It had rained during the afternoon, a slashing tropical downpour that drummed along the deck and pocked the surface of the water like hail, but it was clear now, and the hot stars of the southern latitudes were ablaze across the sky. The *Topaz* was moored stern-to at a low wooden wharf with her anchor out ahead, shadowy in the faint illumination from a lamp a half block away where the row of palms along the street stirred and rustled in the breeze blowing in from the Caribbean.

It was eight p.m. Keefer had gone off to the nearest bar with two or three dollars he had left from the twenty I'd advanced him. I went below to catalogue and stow the charts I had bought. I switched on the overhead light and stood for a moment at the foot of the companion ladder, looking forward. She was all right. She had a good interior layout, and the six-foot-two-inch headroom was adequate.

The small bottled-gas stove and stainless-steel sink of the galley were on the port side aft, with the wooden refrigerator

below and stowage above. To starboard was a settee. Above
it was the RDF and radiotelephone, and a chart table that
folded back when not in use. Just forward of this area were
two permanent bunks, and beyond them a locker to port and
the small enclosed head to starboard. These, and the curtain
between them, formed a passage going into the forward compartment, which was narrower and contained two additional
bunks.

The charts were in a roll on the settee. I cut the cord bind-
ing them, and pulled down the chart table. Switching on the
light above it, I began checking them off against my list,
rolling them individually, and stowing them in the rack overhead. It was hot and very still here below, and sweat dripped
off my face. I mopped at it, thinking gratefully that to-
morrow we would be at sea.

I had a Hydrographic Office general chart of the Caribbean spread out on the table and was lighting a cigarette
when a voice called out quietly from ashore, "Ahoy, aboard
the *Topaz!*"

I stuck my head out the companion hatch. The shadowy
figure on the wharf was tall but indistinct in the faint light,
and I couldn't see the face. But he sounded American, and
judging from the way he'd hailed he could be off one of the
other yachts. "Come on aboard," I invited.

I stepped back, and the man came into view down the
companion ladder—heavy brogues first, and then long legs
in gray flannel slacks, and at last a brown tweed jacket. It
was an odd way to be dressed in Panama, I thought, where
everybody wore white and nothing heavier than linen. The
man's face appeared, and he stood at the foot of the ladder

with his head inclined slightly because of his height. It was
a slender, well-made face, middle-aged but not sagging or
deeply lined, with the stamp of quietness and intelligence
and good manners on it. The eyes were brown. He was bareheaded, and the short-cropped brown hair was graying.

"Mr. Rogers?" he asked politely.

"That's right," I said.

"My name is Baxter. Wendell Baxter."

We shook hands. "Welcome aboard," I said. "How about
some coffee?"

"Thank you, no." Baxter moved slightly to one side of the
companion ladder, but remained standing. "I'll get right to
the point, Mr. Rogers. I heard you were looking for a hand to
take her north."

I was surprised, but concealed it. Baxter had neither the
appearance nor the bearing of one who would be looking for
a job as a paid deckhand. College students, yes; but this man
must be around fifty. "Well, I've already got one man," I
said.

"I see. Then you didn't consider taking two? I mean, to
cut the watches."

"Watch-and-watch does get pretty old," I agreed. "And I
certainly wouldn't mind having two. You've had experience?"

"Yes."

"Offshore? The Caribbean can get pretty lumpy for a
forty-foot yawl."

Baxter had been looking at the chart. He glanced up
quickly, but the brown eyes were merely polite. "Yawl?"

I grinned. "I've had two applicants who called her a

schooner, and one who wanted to know if I planned to anchor every night."

A faint smile touched Baxter's lips. "I see."

"Have you had a chance to look her over?" I asked.

"Yes. I saw her this morning."

"What do you make of her?"

"This is just a guess, of course, but I'd say she was probably an Alden design, and New England built, possibly less
than ten years ago. She seems to have been hauled recently,
probably within two months, unless she's been lying in fresh
water. The rigging is in beautiful shape, except that the
lower shroud on the port side of the main has some broken
strands."

I nodded. I already had the wire aboard to replace that
shroud in the morning before sailing. Baxter was no farmer.
I nodded toward the chart. "What do you think of the
course, the way I've laid it out?"

He studied it for a moment. "If the Trades hold, it should
be a broad reach most of the way. Once you're far enough to
the north'ard to weather Gracias a Dios, you can probably
lay the Yucatán Channel on one course. Do you carry genoa
and spinnaker?"

"No," I said. "Nothing but the working sails. We'll probably be twelve days or longer to Southport, and all I can
offer you is a hundred for the passage. Are you sure you want
to go?"

"The pay isn't important," he replied. "Primarily, I
wanted to save the plane fare."

"You're an American citizen, I suppose."

"Yes. My home's in San Francisco. I came down here

on a job that didn't work out, and I'd like to get back as cheaply as possible."

"I see," I said. I had the feeling somehow that behind the quiet demeanor and well-bred reserve Baxter was tense with anxiety, wanting to hear me say yes. Well, why not? The man was obviously experienced, and it would be well worth the extra hundred not to have to stand six-and-six. "It's a deal, then. Can you be aboard early in the morning? I'd like to get away before ten."

He nodded. "I'll have my gear aboard in less than an hour."

He left, and returned in forty-five minutes carrying a single leather suitcase of the two-suiter variety. "Keefer and I are in these bunks," I said. "Take either of those in the forward compartment. You can stow your bag in the other one."

"Thank you. That will do nicely," he replied. He stowed his gear, removed the tweed jacket, and opened the mushroom ventilator overhead. He came out after a while and sat silently smoking a cigarette while I rated the chronometer with a time signal from WWV.

"I gather you've cruised quite a bit," I said tentatively.

"I used to," he replied.

"In the Caribbean, and West Indies?"

"No. I've never been down here before."

"My normal stamping ground is the Bahamas," I went on. "That's wonderful country."

"Yes. I understand it is." The words were uttered with the same grave courtesy, but from the fact that he said nothing further it was obvious he didn't wish to pursue the discussion.

Okay, I thought, a little hacked about it; you don't have
to talk if you don't want to. I didn't like being placed in the
position of a gossipy old woman who had to be rebuffed for
prying. A moment later, however, I thought better of it and
decided I was being unfair. A man who was down on his
luck at fifty could quite justifiably not wish to discuss his
life story with strangers. Baxter, for all his aloofness, struck
me as a man you could like.

Keefer returned about an hour later. I introduced them.
Baxter was polite and reserved. Keefer, cocky with the beer
he'd drunk and full of the merchant seaman's conviction
that anybody who normally lived ashore was a farmer, was
inclined to be condescending. I said nothing. Blackie was
probably in for a few surprises; I had a hunch that Baxter
was a better sailor than he ever would be. We all turned in
shortly after ten. When I awoke just at dawn, Baxter was
already up and dressed. He was standing beside his bunk,
just visible past the edge of the curtain, using the side of
his suitcase as a desk while he wrote something on a pad of
airmail stationery.

"Why don't you use the chart table?" I asked.

He looked around. "Oh. This is all right. I didn't want to
wake you."

I threw the third cigarette over the side, and stood up and
stretched. There was nothing in any of that except the fact
that Baxter's flannels and tweeds were a little out of place
in Panama. But maybe he merely hadn't wanted to spend
money for tropical clothes, especially if the job had looked
none too permanent.

It was dusk now, and the glow over the city was hot against the sky. I snapped the padlock on the hatch, and walked up to the gate. Johns looked up from his magazine. "Goin' out for supper?"

"Yes. What's a good air-conditioned restaurant that has a bar?"

"Try the Golden Pheasant, on Third and San Benito. You want me to call you a cab?"

I shook my head. "Thanks. I'll walk over and catch the bus."

I crossed the railroad tracks in the gathering darkness and entered the street. The bus stop was one block up and two blocks to the right. It was a district of large warehouses and heavy industry, the streets deserted now and poorly lighted. I turned right at the corner and was halfway up the next block, before a shadowy junkyard piled high with wrecked automobiles, when a car turned into the street behind me, splashing me for an instant with its lights. It swerved to the curb and stopped. "Hey, you," a voice growled.

I turned, and looked into the shadowy muzzle of an automatic projecting from the front window. Above it was an impression of a hatbrim and a brutal outcropping of jaw. "Get in," the voice commanded.

The street was deserted for blocks in each direction. Behind me was the high, impassable fence of the junkyard. I looked at the miles of utter nothing between me and the corner. "All right. The wallet's in my hip pocket—"

"We don't want your wallet. I said get in!" The muzzle of the gun moved almost imperceptibly, and the rear door opened. I stepped toward it. As I leaned down, hands reached out of the darkness inside and yanked. I fell inward. Something slashed down on my left shoulder. My arm went numb to the fingertips. I tried to get up. Light exploded just back of my eyes.

My head was filled with a running groundswell of pain. It rose and fell, and rose again, pressing against my skull in hot waves of orange, and when I opened my eyes the orange gave way to a searing white that made me shudder and close them again. Muscles tightened spasmodically across my abdomen as nausea uncoiled inside me. I was conscious of a retching sound and of the sensation of strangling.

"Prop him up," a bored voice said. "You want him to drown in it?"

I felt myself hauled upward and pushed against something behind me. I retched and heaved again. "Throw some water on him," the voice commanded. "He stinks."

Footsteps went away and came back. Water caught me in the face, forcing my head back and running up my nostrils. I choked. The rest of it splashed onto the front of my shirt. I opened my eyes again. The light burned into them. I reached for it to push it away, but found it was apparently glaring at me from some incalculable distance, because my fingertips could not reach it. Maybe it was the sun. Maybe, on the other hand, I was in hell.

Somewhere in the darkness beyond my own little cosmos of light and pain and the smell of vomit, a voice asked, "Can you hear me, Rogers?"

I tried to say something, but only retched again. More water slapped me in the face. When it had run out of my nose and mouth I tried again. This time I was able to form words. They were short words, and very old ones.

"Rogers, I'm talking to you," the voice said. "Where did you put him ashore?"

I groped numbly around in my mind for some meaning to that, but gave up. "Who? What are you talking about?"

"Wendell Baxter. Where did you put him ashore?"

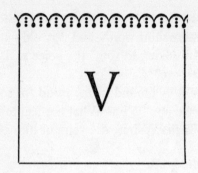

V

"Baxter?" I put a hand up over my eyes to shield them from the light. "Ashore?"

"He couldn't be that stupid." This seemed to be a different voice. Tough, with a rasping inflection. "Let me belt him one."

"Not yet." This was the first one again—incisive, commanding, a voice with four stripes.

A random phrase, torn from some lost context, boiled up through the pain and the jumbled confusion of my thoughts. . . . Professional muscle . . . That policeman had said it. Willard? Willetts? That was it. *Sounds like professional muscle to me.* . . .

"We're going to have to soften him up a little."

"Shut up. Rogers, where did you land him? Mexico? Honduras? Cuba?"

"I don't know what you're talking about," I said.

"We're talking about Wendell Baxter."

"Baxter is dead," I said. "He died of a heart attack—"

"And you buried him at sea. Save it, Rogers; we read the papers. Where is he?"

My head was clearing a little now. I had no idea where I was, but I could make out that I was sitting on a rough wooden floor with my back propped against a wall and that the light glaring in my face was a powerful flashlight held by someone just in front of and above me. Now that I looked under it I could see gray-trousered legs and a pair of expensive-looking brogues. To my right was another pair of shoes, enormous ones, size twelve at least. I looked to the left and saw one more pair. These were black, and almost as large, and the right one had a slit along the welt about where the little toe would be, as if the wearer had a corn. In my groggy state I fastened onto details like that like a baby seeing the world for the first time. Water ran out of my clothing; I was sitting in a puddle of it. My hair and face were still dripping, and when I licked my lips I realized it was salt. We must be on a pier, or aboard a boat.

"Where was Baxter headed?"

Maybe they were insane. "He's dead," I repeated patiently. "We buried him at sea. For God's sake, why would I lie about it?"

"Because he paid you."

I opened my mouth to say something, but closed it. A little chill ran down my spine as I began to understand.

"Let me work him over."

"Not yet, I tell you. You want to scramble his brains again and have to wait another hour? He'll talk. All right, Rogers, do you want me to spell it out for you?"

"I don't care what you spell out. Baxter is dead."

"Listen. Baxter came aboard the *Topaz* on the night of May thirty-first in Cristobal. The three of you sailed the next morning, June first, and you and Keefer arrived here on the sixteenth. Baxter paid you ten thousand dollars to land him somewhere on the coast of Central America, Mexico, or Cuba, and cook up that story about the heart attack and having to bury him at sea—"

"I tell you he died!"

"Shut up till I'm finished. Baxter should have had better sense than to trust a stupid meathead like Keefer. We know all about him. The night before you sailed from Panama he was down to his last dollar, mooching drinks in a waterfront bar. When you arrived here sixteen days later he moved into the most expensive hotel in town and started throwing money around like a drunk with an expense account. They're holding twenty-eight hundred for him in the hotel safe, and he had over six hundred in his wallet when his luck ran out. That figures out to somewhere around four grand altogether, so you must have got more. It was your boat. Where's Baxter now?"

"Lying on the bottom, in about two thousand fathoms," I said hopelessly. What was the use? They'd never believe me; Keefer had fixed that, for all time. I thought of the pulpy mess the gun barrels had made of his face, and shuddered. These were the men who'd done it, and they'd do the same thing to me.

"Okay," the voice said in the darkness beyond the flashlight. "Maybe you'd better prime him a little."

A big arm swung down and the open hand rocked my

face around. I tried to climb to my feet; another hand grabbed the front of my shirt and hauled. I swayed weakly, trying to swing at the shadowy bulk in front of me. My arms were caught from behind. A fist like a concrete block slugged me in the stomach. I bent forward and fell, writhing in agony, when the man behind turned me loose.

"Where's Baxter?"

I was unable to speak. One of them hauled me to a sitting position again and slammed me against the wall. I sobbed for breath while the light fixed me like some huge and malevolent eye.

"Why be stupid?" the voice asked. "All we want to know is where you put him ashore. You don't owe him anything; you carried out your end of the bargain. He's making a sucker of you, anyway; he knew he was letting you in for this, but he didn't tell you that, did he?"

"Then why would I lie about it?" I gasped. "If I'd put him ashore, I'd tell you. But I didn't."

"He promised you more money later? Is that it?"

"He didn't promise me anything, or give me anything. I don't know where Keefer got that money, unless he stole it out of Baxter's suitcase. But I do know Baxter's dead. I sewed him in canvas myself, and buried him."

The rasping voice broke in. "Cut out the crap, Rogers! We're not asking *if* you put him ashore. We know that already, from Keefer. But he didn't know where, because you did all the navigation. It was the mouth of some river, but he didn't know which one, or what country it was in."

"Was this *after* you'd broken all the bones in his face?" I asked. "Or while you were still breaking them? Look, you knew Baxter, presumably. Didn't he ever have a heart attack before?"

"No."

"Is Baxter his right name?"

"Never mind what his name is."

"I take it that it's not. Then why are you so sure the man who was with me is the one you're looking for?"

"He was seen in Panama."

"It could still be a mistake."

"Take a look." A hand extended into the cone of light, holding out a photograph.

I took it. It was a four-by-five snapshot of a man at the topside controls of a sport fisherman, a tall and very slender man wearing khaki shorts and a long-visored fishing cap. It was Baxter; there was no doubt of it. But it was the rest of the photo that caught my attention—the boat itself, and the background. There was something very familiar about the latter.

"Well?" the voice asked coldly.

I held it out. "It's Baxter." Lying was futile.

"Smart boy. Of course it is. You ready to tell us now?"

"I've already told you. He's dead."

"I don't get you, Rogers. I know you couldn't be stupid enough to think we're bluffing. You saw Keefer."

"Yes, I saw him. And what did it buy you? A poor devil out of his mind with pain trying to figure out what you wanted him to say so he could say it. Is that what you want? I'm no braver with a broken face than the next guy, so I'll probably do the same thing."

"We've wasted enough time with him!" This was the tough voice again. "Grab his arms!"

I tried to estimate the distance to the flashlight, and gathered myself. It was hopeless, but I had to do something. I came up with a rush just before the hands reached me, pushing myself off the wall and lunging toward the light. A hand caught my shirt. It tore. The light swung back, but I was on it; it fell to the floor and rolled, but didn't go out. The beam sprayed along the opposite wall. There was an open doorway, and beyond it a pair of mooring bitts, and the dark outline of a barge. A blow knocked me off balance; a hand groped, trying to hold me. I spun away from it, driving toward the door. Shoes scraped behind me, and I heard a grunt and curses as two of them collided in the darkness. Something smashed against the side of my head, and I started to fall. I hit the door frame, pushed off it, and wheeled, somehow still on my feet, and I was in the open. Stars shone overhead, and I could see the dark gleam of water beyond the end of the barge.

I tried to turn, to run along the pier. One of them crashed into me from behind, and tackled me around the waist. Our momentum carried us outward toward the edge. My legs struck one of the mooring lines of the barge, and I shot outward and down, falling between it and the pier.

Water closed over me. I tried to swim laterally before I surfaced, and came up against solid steel. I was against the side of the barge. I kicked off it and brushed against barnacles that sliced into my arm. It was one of the pilings. I grabbed it, pulled around to the other side, and came up.

"Bring the light! Somebody bring the light!" a man was

yelling just above me. Apparently he'd caught the mooring line and saved himself from falling. I heard footsteps pounding on the wooden planking overhead. They'd be able to see me, unless I got back farther under the pier, but the tide was pushing me out, against the barge. I tried to hold onto the piling and see if there was another one farther in that I could reach, but the darkness in that direction was impenetrable. The current was too strong to swim against.

Light burst on the water around me. "There he is! There's the creep!" somebody yelled. "There's his hand!" I took a deep breath and went under, and immediately I was against the side of the barge again. I might swim alongside it for some distance, but when I surfaced I'd still be within range of that light. I did the only thing left. I swam straight down against the side of the barge. My ears began to hurt a little, so I knew I was below twelve feet when the plates bent inward around the turn of the bilge and there was only emptiness below me. It was frightening there in the pitch darkness, not knowing how wide she was or how much water there was under the flat bottom, but it wasn't half as deadly as the three goons back there on the wharf. There was no turning back, anyway; the current was already carrying me under. I kicked hard, and felt the back of my head scrape along the bottom plates.

Then there was mud under my hands. For a moment I almost panicked; then I regained presence of mind enough to know that the only chance I had was to keep on going straight ahead. If I turned now I'd never get out. Even if I didn't lose all sense of direction and get lost completely, I'd never be able to swim back up against the current. I kicked ahead. The water shoaled a little more; my knees were in mud now, with my back scraping along the bottom of the barge.

Suddenly there was only water below me and I was going faster. My lungs began to hurt. I passed the turn of the bilge and shot upward. My head broke surface at last, and I inhaled deeply—once, twice, and then I went under again just as the light burst across the water not ten feet off to my left. They had run across the barge and were searching this side. I stayed under, kicking hard and letting the tide carry me. When I surfaced again I was some fifty yards away. They were still throwing the light around and cursing. I began swimming across the current toward the dark line of the beach. In a little while I felt bottom beneath my hands and stood up. I turned and looked back.

I was a good two hundred yards from the pier and the barge now. The flashlight was coming along the shore in my direction. I eased back out until just my head was above water, and waited. I could hear them talking. When they were almost opposite me, they turned and went back. A few minutes later a car started up, near the landward end of the pier. The twin beams swung in an arc, and I watched the red taillights fade and disappear. I waded ashore in the dark. The reaction hit me all of a sudden, and I was weak and very shaky in the knees, and I had to sit down.

After a while I took off my clothes and squeezed some of the water out of them. I still had my wallet and watch and cigarette lighter. I pressed as much water as I could out of the soggy papers and the money in the wallet and threw away the mushy cigarettes. It was hard getting the wet clothes back on in the darkness. There was no wind, and mosquitoes made thin whining sounds around my ears. Far off to my right I could see the glow of Southport's lights reflected against the sky. I stood up, located Polaris to orient myself, and started walking.

"Where is it?" Willetts asked. "Can you describe the place?"

"Yes," I said. "It must be eight or ten miles west of town. I walked about three before I could flag a patrol car. It's a single wooden pier with a shed on it. There's a steel barge moored to the west side of it. The buildings ashore apparently burned down a long time ago; there's nothing left but foundations and rubble."

He exchanged a glance with Ramirez, and they nodded. "Sounds like the old Bowen sugar mill. It's outside the city limits, but we can go take a look. You better come along and see if you can identify it. You sure you're all right now?"

"Sure," I said.

It was after ten p.m. We were in Emergency Receiving at County Hospital, where the men in the patrol car had brought me. They had radioed in as soon as I gave them the story, and received word back to hold me until it could be investigated. A bored intern checked me over, said I had a bad bruise on the back of my head but no fracture, cleaned the barnacle cuts on my arms, stuck on a few Band-Aids, and gave me a cigarette and two aspirins.

"You'll live," he said, with the medic's vast non-interest in the healthy.

I wondered how long. They'd given up for the moment, but when they found out I hadn't drowned they'd be back.

What should I do? Ask for police protection for the rest of my life? That would be a laugh. A grown man asking protection from three pairs of shoes.

Who was Baxter? Why did they want him? And what in the name of God had given them the idea we had put him ashore? I was still butting my head against the same blank wall twenty minutes later when Willetts and Ramirez showed up. They'd been off duty, of course, but were called in because Keefer was their case. I repeated the story.

"All right, let's go," Willetts said.

We went out and got in the cruiser. Ramirez drove—quite fast, but without using the siren. My clothes were merely damp now, and the cool air was pleasant; the headache had subsided to a dull throbbing. We rode a freeway for a good part of the distance, and the trip took less than fifteen minutes. As soon as we came out to the end of the bumpy and neglected shell-surfaced road and stopped, I recognized it. Willetts and Ramirez took out flashlights and we walked down through the blackened rubble to the pier.

We found the doorway into the shed, opposite the barge. Inside it was black and empty. The floor against the opposite wall was still wet where I'd vomited and they'd thrown water on me, and nearby was the fire bucket they'd used. It had a piece of line made fast to the handle. Willetts took it along to be checked for fingerprints. There was nothing else, no trace of blood or anything to indicate Keefer had been killed there. We went out on the pier. Ramirez shot his light down into the water between the piling and the side of the barge. "And you swam under it? Brother."

"There wasn't much choice at the time," I said.

We went back to the police station, to the office I'd been in that morning. They took down my statement.

"You never did see their faces?" Willetts asked.

"No. They kept that light in my eyes all the time. But there were three of them, and at least two were big and plenty rough."

"And they admitted they killed Keefer?"

"You've got their exact words," I said. "I wouldn't say there was much doubt of it."

"Have you got any idea at all why they're after Baxter?"

"No."

"Or who Baxter really is?"

"Who Baxter really *was*," I said. "And the answer is no."

"But you think now he might be from Miami?"

"At some time in his life, anyway. I don't know how long ago it was, but that picture they showed me was taken on Biscayne Bay. I'm almost positive of it."

"And they didn't give any reason for that idea you'd put him ashore? I mean, except that Keefer turned up with all that money?"

"No."

He lighted a cigarette and leaned across the desk. "Look, Rogers. This is just a piece of advice from somebody who's in the business. Whatever happened in Panama, or out in the middle of the ocean, is out of our jurisdiction and no skin off our tail, but you're in trouble. If you know anything about this you're not telling, you'd better start spilling it before you wind up in an alley with the cats looking at you."

"I don't know a thing about it I haven't told you," I said.

"All right. We have to take your word for it; you're the

only one left, and we've got no real evidence to the contrary. But I can smell these goons. They're pros, and I don't think they're local. I've put the screws on every source I've got around town, and nobody knows anything about 'em at all. Our only chance to get a lead on 'em would be to find out who Baxter was, and what he was up to."

"That's great," I said. "With Baxter buried at the bottom of the Caribbean Sea."

"The thing that puzzles me the most is what the hell he was doing on that boat of yours in the first place. The only way you can account for that money of Keefer's is that he stole it from Baxter. So if Baxter was running from a bunch of hoodlums and had four thousand in cash, why would he try to get away on a boat that probably makes five miles an hour downhill? Me, I'd take something faster."

"I don't know," I said. "It gets crazier every time I look at it. The only thing I'm sure of any more is that I wish to Christ I'd never heard of Baxter *or* Keefer."

"Okay. There's nothing more we can do now. I've got a hunch the FBI is going to want to take a long, slow look at this, but they can pick you up in the morning. We'll send you back to your boat in a squad car. And if you have to go chasing around town at night, for God's sake take a taxi."

"Sure," I said. "They struck me as being scared to death of taxi drivers."

"They're scared of witnesses, wise guy. They all are. And you've always got a better chance where they can't get a good look at you."

It was 12:20 a.m. when the squad car dropped me off before the boatyard gate and drove away. I glanced nervously

up and down the waterfront with its shadows and gloomy
piers and tried to shrug off the feeling of being watched. It
was as peaceful as the open sea, with nobody in sight anywhere except old Ralph, the twelve-to-eight watchman,
tilted back in a chair just inside the gate reading a magazine
in his hot pool of light. He glanced curiously at the police
car and at my muddy shoes, but said nothing. I said good
night, and went on down through the yard. As I stepped
aboard the *Topaz* and walked aft to the cockpit, I reached
in my pocket for the key. Then I saw I wasn't going to need
it.

The hatch was open and the padlock was gone, the hasp
neatly cut through, apparently with bolt cutters. I looked
down into the dark interior of the cabin, and felt the hair
raise along the back of my neck. I listened intently, standing
perfectly still, but knew that was futile. If he was still down
there, he'd heard me already. Well, I could find out. The
light switch was right beside the ladder, accessible from
here. I stepped to one side of the hatch, reached down silently, and flipped it on. Nothing happened. I peered in.
He was gone. But he'd been there. The whole cabin looked
as if it had been stirred with a giant spoon.

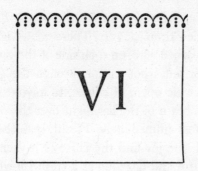

VI

THE BUNKS had been torn apart. The bedding was piled on the settee and in the sink. My suitcase and duffel bag were emptied into the bunks, the drawers beneath them dumped upside down on the deck. Food lockers were emptied and ransacked. Charts, nautical almanacs, azimuth tables, magazines, and books were scattered everywhere. I stared at it in mounting rage. A hell of a security force they had here, one creaky old pensioner sitting up there calmly reading a magazine while thieves tore your boat apart. Then I realized it wasn't his fault, nor Otto's. Whoever had done this hadn't come in the gate, and was no ordinary sneak thief. The watchmen made the round of the yard once every hour with a clock, but there was no station out here on the pier. I grabbed a flashlight and ran back on deck.

The *Topaz* lay near the outer end of the pier, bow in and starboard side to. There was a light at the shoreward end of the pier, but out here it was somewhat shadowy, especially aft. The marine railway and the shrimp boat that was on it blocked the view from the gate. There was a high wire fence, topped with barbed wire, on each side of the yard, so no one could go in or out afoot except through the gate, but the bayfront was wide open, of course, to anyone with a boat.

I threw the beam of the flashlight over the port side, and found it almost immediately. Freshly painted white topsides are both the joy and the curse of a yachtsman's life; they're beautiful and dazzling as a fresh snowfall, and just as easily marred. Right under the cockpit coaming was a slight dent, with green paint in it. Skiff, I thought, or a small outboard; it had bumped as it came alongside. If they had a motor, they had probably cut it some distance out and sculled in. Probably happened on Otto's watch, right after I left. That meant, then, that there were at least four of them. But what were they looking for?

I was just straightening up when I saw something else. I stopped the light and looked again to make sure. There was another dent, about ten feet forward of this one. What the hell, had they come alongside at twenty knots and ricocheted? I stepped forward and knelt to have a closer look. There was a smear of yellow paint in this one. *Two boats?* That made no sense at all. One of the dents must have been made before, I thought. But it couldn't have been very long ago, because it was only Thursday I'd painted the topsides.

Well, it didn't make any difference. The point was that they'd been here, and they could come back. If I wanted to get any sleep I'd better move to a hotel; this place was too easy to get into. I went below and straightened up the mess. So far as I could tell, nothing was missing. I changed into a lightweight suit—the only one I had with me—put on some more shoes, and packed a bag with the rest of my gear. I gathered up the sextant and chronometer, the only valuable items aboard, and went up to the gate.

The old man was shocked and apologetic and a little frightened when I told him about it. "Why, I didn't hear a thing, Mr. Rogers," he said.

"It probably happened on Otto's shift," I said. "But it doesn't matter; nobody would have heard them, anyway. Just keep this chronometer and sextant in your shack till Froelich gets here in the morning." Froelich was the yard foreman. "Turn them over to him, and tell him to put a new hasp and padlock on that hatch. At yard expense, incidentally. And tell him not to let anybody down in the cabin until the police have a chance to check it for fingerprints. I'll be back around nine o'clock."

"Yes, sir," he said. "I'll sure do that. And I'm awful sorry about it, Mr. Rogers."

"Forget it," I told him. I called the police and reported it, with a request that they notify Willetts when he came on shift again. This had to be explained, because Willetts was in Homicide and had nothing to do with burglary. We got it straightened out at last, and I called a cab. The driver recommended the Bolton as a good commercial hotel.

I watched the empty streets as we drove through the warehouse and industrial district. No one followed us. Even the thought of violence seemed unreal. The Bolton was in the heart of the downtown business district, about three blocks from the Warwick. It was air-conditioned. I registered, and followed the boy through the deserted corridors of two a.m., reminded of the description of a hotel in one of Faulkner's novels. *Tiered cubicles of sleep.* The room was a cubicle, all right, but it had a night latch and a chain on the door. When the boy had gone I slipped the chain in place, took a shower, and lay down on the bed with a cigarette.

Who was Baxter?

He's a legacy, I thought. An incubus I inherited, with an assist from Keefer. Baxter to Keefer to Rogers—it sounded like the infield of a sandlot baseball team. Why had he come aboard the *Topaz?* He'd obviously lied about the job and about wanting to save plane fare home. He hadn't struck me as a liar, either; aloof, maybe, and close-mouthed, but not a liar. And certainly not a criminal. I'd liked him.

Who were the men after him? And why wouldn't they believe he had died of a heart attack? And just what did I do now? Spend the rest of my life looking under the bed, sleeping behind locked doors on the upper floors of hotels? It was chilling when you thought of it, how little the police could actually do about a thing like this, unless I wanted to go down there and live in the squad room and never go out at all. And trying to convince myself that I was any match for professional hoodlums was farcical. Violence was their business. It wasn't a sport, like football, with rules, and time out when you got hurt. Even if I had a gun and a permit to carry it, it would be useless; I was no gunman, and didn't want to be one.

I lighted another cigarette, and looked at my watch. It was almost three a.m.

The only way to get a line on them, Willetts had said,

was to find out who Baxter was. And since the physical remains of Baxter were buried beyond the reach of the human race for eternity, the only thing left was trailing him backward in search of some clue. That, obviously, was a job for the FBI. But so far the FBI didn't even have a place to start. I had four days.

Take it from where you left off, I thought: the morning we sailed. After breakfast the three of us had turned to, replacing the stainless-steel lower shroud on the port side of the mainmast. Baxter was a willing worker and he was good with wire, but his hands were soft and he apparently had no gloves. I noted also that he was working in the pair of gray flannel slacks. While we were still at it, the stores came down. We carried them aboard and stowed them. There was a discrepancy in the bill that I wanted to take up with the ship chandler, so I asked the driver for a ride back to town in the truck. Just as I was going ashore, Baxter came up from below and called to me.

He handed me twenty dollars. "I wonder if you'd mind getting me two pairs of dungarees while you're uptown? The stores were closed last night."

"Sure," I said. "What size?"

"Thirty-two waist, and the longest they have."

"Right. But why not come along yourself? We're in no bind."

He declined apologetically. "Thanks, but I'd just as soon stay and finish that wire. That is, if you don't mind getting the dungarees."

I told him I didn't. He took an airmail letter from his pocket and asked if I'd drop it in the box for him—

Paula Stafford!

I sat up in bed so suddenly I dropped my cigarette and had to retrieve it from the floor. That's where I'd heard the name. Or had seen it, rather. When I was mailing the letter I'd noticed idly that it was addressed to somebody at a hotel in New York. I wasn't prying; it was merely that the New York address had struck me, since he was from San Francisco, and I'd glanced at the name. *Stanford? Sanford? Stafford?* That was it; I was positive of it.

God, what a dope! I'd forgotten all about her call. She was probably over at the Warwick Hotel right now, and could clear up the whole mystery in five minutes. I grabbed the telephone.

I waited impatiently while the operator dialed. "Good morning," a musical voice said. "Hotel Warwick."

"Do you have a Paula Stafford registered?" I asked.

"One moment, please. . . . Yes, sir. . . ."

"Would you ring her, please?"

"I'm sorry, sir. Her line is busy."

Probably trying to get me at the boatyard, I thought. I sprang up and began throwing on my clothes. It was only three blocks to the Warwick. The traffic lights were blinking amber, and the streets were empty except for a late bus or two and a Sanitation Department truck. I made it to the Warwick in three minutes. The big ornate lobby was at the bottom of its day's cycle; all the shops were closed, and some of the lights were turned off around the outlying areas with only the desk and switchboard and one elevator still functioning, like the nerve centers of some complex animal asleep. I headed for the house phones, over to the right of the desk.

She answered almost immediately, as if she had been standing beside the instrument. "Yes?"

"Miss Stafford?" I asked.

"Yes," she said eagerly. "Who is it?"

"Stuart Rogers. I'm down in the lobby—"

"Oh, thank Heavens!" She sounded slightly hysterical. "I've been trying to get you at that shipyard, but the man said you were gone, he didn't know where. But never mind. Where are you?"

"Down in the lobby," I repeated.

"Come on up! Room 1508."

It was to the right, the boy said. I stepped out of the elevator and went along a hushed and deep-carpeted corridor. When I knocked, she opened the door immediately. The first thing that struck me about her were her eyes. They were large and deeply blue, with long dark lashes, but they were smudged with sleeplessness and jittery with some intense emotion too long sustained.

"Come in, Mr. Rogers!" She stepped back, gave me a nervous but friendly smile that was gone almost before it landed, and shook a pill out of the bottle she was holding in her left hand. She was about thirty-five, I thought. She had dark hair that was a little mussed, as if she'd been running her hands through it, and was wearing a blue dressing gown, belted tightly about her waist. Paula Stafford was a very attractive woman, aside from an impression that if you dropped something or made a sudden move she might jump into the overhead light fixture.

I came on into the room and closed the door while she grabbed up a tumbler of water from the table on her left and swallowed the pill. Also on the table was a burning cigarette in a long holder, balanced precariously on the edge, another bottle of pills of a different color, and an unopened pint bottle of Jack Daniel's. To my left was the partly opened door of the bathroom. Beyond her was a large double bed with a persimmon-colored spread. The far wall was almost all window, covered with a drawn venetian blind and persimmon drapes. Light came from the bathroom door and from the floor lamp beside the dresser, which was beyond the foot of the bed, to my left. A dress, apparently the one she'd been wearing, was thrown across the bed, along with a half slip, her handbag, and a pair of sun glasses, while her suitcase was open and spilling lingerie and stockings on the luggage stand at the foot of it. It was hard to tell whether she'd taken up residence in the room or had been lobbed into it just before she went off.

"Tell me about him!" she demanded. "Do you think he's all right?" Then, before I could open my mouth, she broke off with another nervous smile and indicated the armchair near the foot of the bed, at the same time grabbing up the bottle of Jack Daniel's and starting to fumble with the seal. "Forgive me. Won't you sit down? And let me pour you a drink."

I lifted the bottle of whisky out of her hands before she could drop it, and placed it on the table. "Thanks, I don't want a drink. But I would like some information."

She didn't even hear me, apparently, or notice that I'd taken the whisky away. She went right on talking. ". . . half out of my mind, even though I know there must be some perfectly good reason he hasn't got in touch with me yet."

"Who?" I asked.

This got through to her. She stopped, looked at me in surprise, and said, "Why, Brian—I mean, Wendell Baxter."

It was my turn this time. It seemed incredible she didn't know. I felt rotten about having to break it to her this way. "I'm sorry, Miss Stafford, but I took it for granted you'd read about it in the papers. Wendell Baxter is dead."

She smiled. "Oh, of course! How stupid of me." She turned away, and began to rummage through her handbag on the bed. "I must say he made no mistake in trusting you, Mr. Rogers."

I stared blankly at the back of her head, and took out a cigarette and lighted it. There was a vague impression somewhere in my mind that her conversation—if that was what it was—would make sense if only you had the key to it.

"Oh, here it is," she said, and turned back with a blue airmail envelope in her hand. I felt a little thrill as I saw the Canal Zone postmark; it was the one I'd mailed for him. At last I might find out something. "This should clear up your doubts as to who I am. Go ahead and read it."

I slid out the letter.

CRISTOBAL, C.Z.
JUNE 1ST

Dearest Paula:

There is time for just the briefest of notes. Slidell is here in the Zone and has seen me. He has the airport covered, but I have found a way to slip out.

I am writing this aboard the ketch *Topaz*, which is sailing shortly for Southport, Texas. I have engaged to go along as deckhand, using the name of Wendell Baxter. They may find out, of course, but I might not be aboard when she arrives. As soon as we are safely at sea I am going to approach Captain Rogers about putting me ashore somewhere farther up the Central American coast. Of course it is possible he won't do it, but I hope to convince him. The price may be high, but fortunately I still have something over $23,000 in cash with me. I shall write again the moment I am ashore, either in Southport or somewhere in Central America. Until then, remember I am safe, no matter what you might hear, and that I love you.

Brian

Twenty-three thousand dollars . . . I stood there dumbly while she took the letter from my fingers, folded it, and slid it back into the envelope.

She looked up at me. "Now," she cried out eagerly, "where is he, Mr. Rogers?"

I had to say something. She was waiting for an answer. "He's dead. He died of a heart attack—"

She cut me short with a gesture of exasperation, tinged with contempt. "Aren't you being a little ridiculous? You've read the letter; you know who I am. Where did you put him ashore? Where was he going?"

I think that was the moment I began to lose my head. It was the utter futility of it. I caught her arms. "Listen! Was Baxter insane?"

"Insane? What are you talking about?"

"Who is Slidell? What does he want?"

"I don't know," she said.

"*You don't know?*"

She jerked her arms free and moved back from me. "He never told me. Slidell was only one of them, but I don't know what he wanted."

"Has anybody read this letter except me?"

"Mr. Rogers, are *you* crazy? Of course nobody else has seen it."

"Well, look," I went on, "do you think he had twenty-three thousand dollars with him?"

"Yes. Of course he did. But why are you asking all these questions? And why don't you answer mine? Where is he?"

"I keep trying to tell you," I said. "He died of a heart attack four days after we left Cristobal. And in those four days he never said anything at all about wanting to be put ashore. I made an inventory of his personal effects, and he didn't have any twenty-three thousand dollars. He had about a hundred and seventy-five. Either Baxter was insane, or we're not even talking about the same man."

Her face became completely still then. She stared at me, her eyes growing wider and wider. "You killed him," she whispered. "That's why I've never heard from him."

"Stop it!" I commanded. "There has to be some answer—"

"You killed him!" She put her hands up alongside her temples and screamed, with the cords standing out in her throat. "You killed him! *You killed him!*"

"Listen!"

She went on screaming. Her eyes were completely mad. I ran.

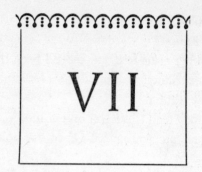

VII

Doors were opening along the corridor and faces were peering out. When I reached the elevator it was on its way up. That would be the hotel detective. I plunged down the stairs with the screams still ringing in my ears. When I reached the lobby at last, it was quiet. Hotels in the Warwick's class don't like police milling around in the lobby if they can help it. I crossed the deserted acres, feeling the eyes of the clerk on my back. In less than five minutes I was back in my own room at the Bolton. I hooked the chain on the door and collapsed on the side of the bed. I reached for a cigarette and got it going somehow.

Now what? There was no use trying to talk to her again; she was on the ragged edge of a crackup. Even if they got her calmed down, seeing me would only set her off again. The thing to do was call the FBI. Then I thought of the letter. If they ever saw that . . .

It was absolutely deadly; the more I looked at it, the

worse it became. How could anybody ever believe me now? Baxter had sailed on the *Topaz* with $23,000 and had never been seen again. I swore he'd died of a heart attack and that all the money he'd had was $175. Then Keefer was discovered to have $4000 nobody could explain, and *he* was killed. I was the only survivor. There was only my unsupported word that Baxter had even had a heart attack, and $19,000 was still missing.

The least I would be suspected of would be stealing from a dead man and then burying him at sea and destroying his identification to cover up the theft. Or landing him on the coast of Central America as he'd asked, and swearing to a false report that he was dead. The third was even worse. Keefer and I could have killed him. Maybe they couldn't convict me of any of it—they wouldn't have any more actual proof on their side than I had on mine—but even the suspicion would ruin me. I was in the charter business. *Cruise the exotic Bahamas with Captain Rogers, and disappear.* They'd take away my license. Except of course that the hoodlums who were after Baxter might kill me before any of these other things could happen. I sat on the side of the bed with my head in my hands.

Then I was struck by an odd thought. What had given *them* the idea I'd put Baxter ashore? It seemed now there was some basis for their insane theory, but how had they known it? So far as I knew he'd written only that one letter, and she swore nobody else had seen it.

I closed my eyes, and I could see Baxter. Baxter at the wheel, watching the compass, looking aloft for the flutter at the luff of the mains'l, Baxter trimming and starting the sheets, Baxter washing dishes, Baxter quietly smoking a cigarette and looking out across the darkening sea at dusk. He haunted me. He was becoming an obsession. If he'd meant what he had written to Paula Stafford, why had he never once, in all those four days, brought up the subject of being put ashore? I wouldn't have done it, of course, but there was no way he could have been sure of that until he'd dangled the proposition and the money in front of me. Why had he changed his mind? If he'd had $23,000, where was it? Maybe Keefer had stolen $4000 of it, but why stop there?

He'd had four whole days in which to bring up the subject, but he never had. Why? Something must have changed his mind, but what? For one agonizing instant I had the feeling that I knew the answer to that, and that I should know who Baxter really was. Then the whole thing was gone. I wanted to beat my fists against my head.

All right, I thought angrily, what did I know about him? Add it all up. He was from Miami, or had been in Miami at some time. I was from Miami myself, and knew a lot of people there, especially around the waterfront. His first name was Brian. The photograph had showed him at the topside controls of a sport fisherman, which was definitely a clue because I had an idea of the type and had seen the last two letters of the name. Maybe I'd seen him somewhere before, or had heard of him. Why not go back to Miami now, instead of sitting here like a duck in a shooting gallery? I reached for the phone.

There were two airlines with service from here to Florida.

The first had nothing available before 12:30 p.m. I called the other.

"Yes, sir," the girl at the reservations desk said, "we still have space on flight 302. That departs Southport five-fifty-five a.m., and arrives Miami at one-forty-five p.m., with stops at New Orleans and Tampa."

I looked at my watch. It was twenty minutes of five. "Right," I said. "The name is Stuart Rogers. I'll pick up the ticket at the airport as soon as I can get there."

I broke the connection and got the hotel operator again. "Give me long distance, please."

When the long-distance operator came on, I said, "I'd like to put in a call to Miami." I gave her the number.

"Thank you. Will you hold on, please?"

I waited, listening to the chatter of the operators. Bill Redmond would love being hauled out of bed this time of morning. He was an old friend—we'd been classmates at the University of Miami—but he was a reporter on the *Herald*, and had probably just got to sleep. The *Herald* is a morning paper.

"Hello." It was a girl's voice. A very sleepy girl.

"I have a long distance call from Southport, Texas—" the operator began.

"I don't know any Texans—"

"Lorraine," I broke in, "this is Stuart."

"Oh, good God. Bachelors! There ought to be a law."

"Will you put Bill on? It's important."

"I'll bet. Well, stand back, and I'll poke him with something."

I heard him mutter drowsily. Then, "Look, pal, you got any idea what time it is?"

"Never mind," I said. "You can sleep when you get old. I need some help. It's about that trip up from Cristobal with that ketch I went down there to buy."

He interrupted, fully awake now. "I know about it. AP carried a few lines, and we ran it on account of the local angle. Guy died of a heart attack, what was his name?"

"That's it exactly," I said. "What was his name? It was supposed to be Baxter, but it turns out that was phony. There was something wrong about him, and I'm in a hell of a jam I'll tell you about as soon as I can get there. I've got to find out who he was. I think he was from Miami, and there's some sort of screwy impression I've heard of him before. Are you still with me?"

"Keep firing. What did he look like?"

I gave him a short description, and went on. "The Miami hunch comes from a photograph of him that was shown me. I'm pretty sure what I saw in the background was part of the MacArthur Causeway and some of those islands along Government Cut. He was on the flying bridge of a sport fisherman. It was a big one and expensive looking, and I think it was one of those Rybovich jobs. If he owned it, he was probably well-heeled when he was around there because they're not exactly the playthings of the Social Security set. One of the life rings was just behind him, and I could see the last two letters of the name. They were 'a-t.' From the size of the letters, it could be a long name. His first name was Brian. B-r-i-a-n. Got all that?"

"Yeah. And I'm like you. I think I hear a bell trying to ring."

"There was also mention of another man I don't know anything about at all. Slidell. Maybe somebody's heard of him. I'll be in Miami as soon as I can get there. See if you can find out anything at all."

"Right. Take it easy, sailor."

Packing was no problem; I hadn't unpacked. I called the desk to get my bill ready and send for a cab. The lobby was empty except for the clerk. I settled the bill and was putting away my change when the taxi driver came in and got the bag. We went out. It was growing light now. The street had been washed, and for this brief moment just at dawn the city was almost cool and fresh. I looked up and down the street; there were no pedestrians in sight, and only an occasional car. "Airport," I told the driver, and we pulled out.

I watched out the rear window, and just before we reached the end of the block I saw a car pull out from the curb behind us. It had its lights on, so it was impossible to get an idea of what make it was, or what color. Two blocks ahead we turned to the left. The car—or another one —was still behind us. I kept watching. For a time there were two, and then three, and then we were back to one again. There was no way to tell if it was the same one, but it always stayed the same distance back, about a full city block. We made another turn, picking up the highway leading out of town, and it was still there.

I began to worry. The airport was pretty far out, and there were no doubt plenty of deserted stretches of road where they could force us off if they were after me. My only chance—if I had any—would be to jump and run for it. I'd have to warn the driver, though. If he tried to outrun them, they'd probably kill him. The minute I saw them start to close in, I'd tell him to stop.

Then, suddenly, they turned off and we were alone. After another mile with the pavement completely empty behind us, I heaved a sigh of relief. False alarm. I was too jittery. Hell, they didn't even know I was at the hotel; nobody had followed us when I came uptown from the boatyard.

Then I realized I was a baby at this sort of thing and that I was up against professionals. Maybe they had been following us. By the time we'd reached the place where they had turned off it was obvious where I was headed, so they no longer had to stay in sight. It could have been the same thing when I came up from the yard. They'd merely called the hotels until they located me; there probably weren't over half a dozen. I felt ridiculous and stupid, and a little scared.

If they were after me, what was the best plan? I remembered what Willetts had said—they're all afraid of witnesses. Then stay in the open, surrounded by plenty of people, I thought. We left the city behind, rolling through the outlying housing developments, and crossed a bayou overhung with dark liveoaks and dangling pennants of Spanish moss. The sun was just rising when we pulled up in front of the airport passenger terminal. I paid off the driver and went inside with my bag.

It was a good-sized terminal, busy even at this hour in the morning. Long windows in front looked out toward

the runways, and at either end were the concourses leading to the gates. To the left were some shops and the
newsstand and restaurant, while all the airline counters
were strung out along the right. I went over, checked in,
and paid for my ticket.

"Thank you, Mr. Rogers," the girl said. She clipped my
luggage check to the boarding pass and gave me my change.
"Concourse B, Gate Seven. The flight will be called in approximately ten minutes."

I bought a newspaper, moved back to a leather-cushioned
bench, and sat down to sweat out the ten minutes. If they
were following me, they'd try to get on this flight, or at
least get one man on it. I was just in back of the two lines
checking in. I looked them over cautiously while pretending to read the paper. There was a slight, graying man with
a flyrod case. Two young girls, who might be teachers on
vacation. An elderly woman. A fat man carrying a briefcase.
A Marine. Two sailors in whites. A squat, heavy-shouldered
man carrying his coat over his arm. My eyes stopped, and
came back to him.

He was at the head of the line now, in the row in which
I'd checked in. He would have been about two places be-
hind me, I thought. The girl was shaking her head at him.
I strained to hear what she was saying.

". . . sold out. We'd be glad to put you on stand-by,
though; there are still about four who haven't checked in."

He nodded. I could see nothing but his back.

"Your name, please?" the girl asked.

"J. R. Bonner."

The voice was a gravelly baritone, but there was none of

the rasp and menace there'd been in the other. Well, why should there be, under the circumstances? You couldn't tell much about a voice from one or two words, anyway. I glanced down at his shoes. They were black, size ten or eleven, but I was a little to the left and couldn't see the outside of the right one. I returned to my paper, pretending to read. In a moment he turned away from the counter. I looked at him in the unseeing, incurious way your eyes go across anyone in a crowd.

Aside from an impression of almost brutal strength about the shoulders and arms, he could have been anybody—line coach of a professional football team, or the boss of a heavy construction outfit. He wore a soft straw hat, white shirt, and blue tie, and the coat he carried over his arm and the trousers were the matching components of a conservative blue suit. He was somewhere around forty, about five-nine, and well over two hundred pounds, but he walked as lightly as a big cat. His eyes met mine for an instant with the chill, impersonal blankness of outer space, and moved on. He sat down on the bench over to my left. I looked back at my paper. How did you know? What did appearances mean? He could be a goon with the accomplished deadliness of a cobra, or he might be wondering at the moment whether to buy his five-year-old daughter a stuffed bear or one of the Dr. Seuss books for a coming-home present. I glanced at his feet again, and this time I could see it. The right shoe had been slit along the welt for about an inch just under the little toe.

I folded the paper, slapped it idly against my hand, and got up and walked past him. He paid no attention. I strolled over and looked out the long glass wall in front at the runways and dead grass and the bright metal skin of a DC-7 shattering the rays of morning sunlight. It was a weird sensation, and a scary one, being hunted. And in broad daylight, in a busy, peaceful airport. It was unreal. But what was even more unreal was the fact that there was nothing I could do about it. Suppose I called the police. Arrest that man; he's got a cut place in his shoe.

I wondered if he had a gun. There didn't seem to be any place he could be carrying one unless he had it in the pocket of the coat slung over his arm. If he held it just right, nobody could tell. He had no luggage. And the chances were he was alone. With the flight sold out there wasn't much percentage in more than one of them bucking the stand-by list. If he got aboard, he could keep me in sight until the others caught up. Well, he wasn't aboard yet. Maybe he wouldn't make it. They announced the flight. I walked out Concourse B, feeling his eyes in the middle of my back in spite of the fact that I knew he probably wasn't even looking at me. Why should he? He knew where I was going.

Number 302 was a continuing flight, so there were only nine or ten people at Gate 7 waiting to go aboard. Some through passengers who had deplaned to stretch their legs were allowed to go through first. Boarding passengers went through single file while the gate attendant checked our tickets. I was last. As I went up the steps I resisted an impulse to look back. He would be watching from somewhere to be sure I went aboard. There were still four or five empty seats, but that meant nothing. Two would be for the stewardesses, and some of the through passengers might still be in the terminal. I took one on the aisle, aft of the door. There might even be people ahead of him on stand-by. I waited. I was on the wrong side to see the gate, even if I'd had a window seat. It was stifling with the plane on the ground. Sweat gathered on my face. Another passenger came aboard, a woman. Then one in uniform, an Air Force major. I began to hope. The captain and first officer came through the doorway and went forward. The door to the flight compartment closed. Then two minutes before they took away the ramp Bonner came through the door. He took the last empty seat.

We were down in the steamy heat of New Orleans at 8:05 for a twenty-minute stop. Bonner played it very cagey; I remained in my seat while the first wave deplaned, but he went out with them. I could see the beauty of that. He could watch the ramp from inside the terminal to see if I got off or not, so he had me bottled up without being in evidence himself. But if he stayed and I got off, five minutes later he would have to follow me. Smart, I thought. I left the plane. As soon as I was inside the terminal I saw him. He was reading a newspaper, paying no attention to me. I sauntered out front to the limousines and taxis. There he was, still paying no attention.

There was no longer any doubt. Maybe I could call the police and have him picked up. No, that wouldn't work. I had no proof whatever. He would have identification, a good story, an alibi—they couldn't hold him ten minutes. I had to escape from him some way. But how? He was a professional and knew all the tricks; I was an amateur.

Then I began to have an idea. Make it novice against novice, and I might have a chance.

We landed at Tampa at 11:40 a.m. As soon as the door was open I arose and stretched and followed the crowd into the terminal. I stood for a moment looking idly at the paperback books in the rack at the newsstand, and then drifted outside. I'd had a forlorn hope that I might catch the taxi stand with only one cab on station, but there was no such luck. There were four. The driver of the lead-off hack, however, was behind the wheel and ready to go. Bonner was just coming through the door about twenty feet to my left, lighting a cigarette and looking at everything except me. I strolled on past the line until I was abreast the lead one.

Turning quickly, I opened the door and slid in. "Downtown. Tampa," I told the driver.

"Yes, sir." He punched the starter. We pulled away from the loading zone. As we headed for the street I looked back. Bonner was climbing into the second cab. We had a lead of about a block. I took a twenty from my wallet and dropped it on the front seat beside the driver.

"There's a cab following us," I said. "Can you lose him?"

His eyes flicked downward at the money and then straight ahead. "Not if he's a cop."

"He's not."

"That's what you say."

"Why would he take a cab?" I asked. "There's a sheriff's car right there at the terminal."

He nodded. Swinging into the street, he bore down on the accelerator. "Mister, consider him lost."

I looked back. The other cab was weaving through traffic slightly less than a block behind us now. We wouldn't have a chance, I thought, if he had one of his fellow professionals at the wheel, but now the odds were even. No, they were a little better than even. We knew what we were going to do, but he had to wait till we'd done it to find out. It took less than ten minutes. The second time we ran a light on the amber and he tried to follow us through on the red, he locked fenders with a panel truck in the middle of the intersection.

"Nice going," I said. "Now the Greyhound Bus terminal."

I got out there and paid him for the meter in addition to the twenty. As soon as he was out of sight, I walked through the station and over to a taxi stand in front of a hotel, and took another cab to a Hertz agency. Thirty minutes later I was headed south on US 41 in a rented Chevrolet. There was no telling how long my luck would last, but for the moment I'd lost them.

My head began to ache again and I was having trouble staying awake. I suddenly realized it was Sunday afternoon now and I hadn't been to bed since Friday night. When I reached Punta Gorda I pulled into a motel and slept for six hours. I rolled into Miami shortly after 2 a.m. Going out to the airport to claim my bag would be too dangerous, even if I got a porter to pick it up. Bonner would be there, or he'd have somebody watching it. I turned the car in, and took a cab to a hotel on Biscayne Boulevard, explained that my bag had got separated from me when I changed planes in Chicago, and registered as Howard Summers from Portland, Oregon. They wouldn't locate me this time merely by calling the hotels. I asked for a room overlooking Bayfront Park, bought a *Herald*, and followed the boy into the elevator. The room was on the twelfth floor. As soon as he left I went over to the window and parted the slats of the venetian blind. Just visible around to the left was City Yacht Basin. Sticking up out of the cluster of sightseeing and charter fishing boats were the tall sticks of the *Orion*. It made me sick to be this near and not be able to go aboard.

I turned away and reached for the telephone. Bill Redmond should be home by now. He answered on the first ring.

"Stuart—" I began.

He cut me off. "Good God, where are you?"

I told him the hotel. "Room 1208."

"*You're in Miami?* Don't you ever read the papers?"

"I've got a *Herald*, but I haven't looked at—"

"Read it. I'm on my way over there now." He hung up.

The paper was lying on the bed, where I'd tossed it when I came in. I spread it open, put a cigarette in my mouth, and started to flick the lighter. Then I saw it.

LOCAL YACHT CAPTAIN
SOUGHT IN SEA MYSTERY

The police had Baxter's letter.

VIII

It was datelined Southport.

The aura of mystery surrounding the voyage of the ill-fated yacht *Topaz* deepened today in a strange new development that very nearly claimed the life of another victim.

Still in critical condition in a local hospital this afternoon following an overdose of sleeping pills was an attractive brunette tentatively identified as Miss Paula Stafford of New York, believed by police to have been close to Wendell Baxter, mysterious figure whose death or disappearance while en route from Panama to Southport on the *Topaz* has turned into one of the most baffling puzzles of recent years. . . .

I plunged ahead, skipping the parts of it I knew. It was continued in a back section. I riffled through it, scattering the pages, and went on. Then I sat down and read the whole thing through again.

It was all there. The hotel detective had gone up to her room shortly after 3:30 a.m. when guests in adjoining rooms reported a disturbance. He found her wildly upset and crying out almost incoherently that somebody had been killed. Since there were no evidences of violence and it was obvious no one else was there, dead or otherwise, he had got her calmed down and left her after she'd taken one of her sleeping pills. At 10 a.m., however, when they tried to call her and could get no response, they entered the room with a pass key and found her unconscious. A doctor was called. He found the remaining pills on the table beside the bed, and had her taken to a hospital. It wasn't known whether the overdose was accidental or a suicide attempt, since no note could be found, but when police came to investigate they found the letter from Baxter. Then everything hit the fan.

My visit came out. The elevator boy and night clerk gave the police my description. They went looking for me, and I'd disappeared from the boatyard. The letter from Baxter was printed in full. There was a rehash of the whole story up to that time, including Keefer's death and the unexplained $4000.

Now apparently $19,000 more was missing, I was missing, and nobody had an idea at all as to what had really happened to Baxter.

> . . . in light of this new development, the true identity of Wendell Baxter is more deeply shrouded in mystery than ever. Police refuse to speculate as to whether or not Baxter might even still be alive. Lieu-

tenant Boyd parried the question by saying, "There is obviously only one person who knows the answer to that, and we're looking for him."

Local agents of the Federal Bureau of Investigation had no comment other than a statement that Captain Rogers was being sought for further questioning.

I pushed the paper aside and tried the cigarette again. This time I got it going. The letter itself wasn't bad enough, I thought; I had to make it worse by running. That's the way it would look; the minute I read it I took off like a goosed gazelle. By this time they would have traced me to the Bolton and then to the airport. And I'd rented the car in Tampa under my own name, and then turned it in here. As soon as the man in the Hertz agency read the paper he'd call them; the taxi driver would remember bringing me to the hotel. Then it occurred to me I was already thinking like a fugitive. Well, I was one, wasn't I? There was a light knock on the door.

I went over. "Who is it?"

"Bill."

I let him in and closed the door. He sighed and shook his head. "Pal, when you get in a jam, you're no shoestring operator."

We're the same age and about the same height, and we've known each other since we were in the third grade. He's thin, restless, blazingly intelligent, somewhat cynical, and one of the world's worst hypochondriacs. Women consider him handsome, and he probably is. He has a slender reckless face, ironic blue eyes, and dark hair that's prematurely graying. He smokes three packs of cigarettes a day, and quits every other week. He never drinks. He's an AA.

"All right," he said, "let's have it."

I told him.

He whistled softly. Then he said, "Well, the first thing is to get you out of here before they pick you up."

"Why?" I asked. "If the FBI is looking for me, maybe I'd better turn myself in. At least they won't kill me. The others will."

"It can wait till morning, if that's what you decide. In the meantime I've got to talk to you. About Baxter."

"Have you got any lead on him at all?" I asked.

"I'm not sure," he said. "That's the reason I've got to talk to you. What I've come up with is so goofy if I tried to tell the police they might have me committed. Let's go."

"Where?" I asked.

"Home, you goof. Lorraine's scrambling some eggs and making coffee."

"Sure. Harboring a fugitive's just a harmless prank. Be our guest in charming, gracious Atlanta."

"Oh, cut it out, Scarface. How would I know you're a fugitive? I never read anything but the *Wall Street Journal*."

I gave in, but insisted we leave the hotel separately. He told me where the car was, and left. I waited five minutes before following. The streets were deserted. I climbed in, and he swung onto Biscayne Boulevard, headed south. They lived close to downtown, in a small apartment house on Brickell Avenue. From habit, I looked out the rear window. As far as I could tell, nobody was following us.

"The Stafford woman's still alive, the last we got," he said, "but they haven't been able to question her yet."

"I've got a sad hunch she doesn't know too much about him, anyway," I said. "She told me she didn't know who those men were, or what they wanted, and I think she was telling the truth. I'm beginning to doubt Baxter even existed; I think he's an hallucination people start seeing just before they crack up."

"You haven't heard anything yet," he said. "When I tell you what I've come up with you'll think we're both around the bend."

"Well, be mysterious about it," I said sourly. "That's just what I need."

"Wait'll we get inside." He swung into a driveway between shadowy palms and parked beside the building. It had only four apartments, each with its own entrance. Theirs was the lower left. We came back around the hibiscus-bordered walk, and went in the front. The living room was dim and quiet, and cool from the air-conditioner. There were no lights on, but there was enough illumination from the kitchen to find our way past the hi-fi and record albums and rows and stacks of books, and the lamps and statuary Lorraine had made. She does ceramics.

At the moment she was scrambling eggs, a long-legged brunette with a velvety tan, rumpled dark brown hair, and wide, humorous, gray eyes. She was wearing Bermuda shorts and sandals, and a white shirt that was pulled together and knotted around her waist. Beyond the stove was a counter with a yellow formica top and tall yellow stools, a small breakfast nook, and a window hung with yellow curtains.

She stopped stirring the eggs long enough to kiss me and wave a hand toward the counter. "Park it, Killer. What's this rumble you're hot?"

"Broads," Bill said. "Always nosy." He set a bottle of bourbon and a glass on the counter in front of me. His theory was that nobody could be sure he didn't drink if there was none around. I poured a big slug and downed it, had a sip of scalding black coffee, and began to feel better. Lorraine put the eggs on the table and sat down across from me, rested her elbows on the counter, and grinned.

"Let's face it, Rogers. Civilization just isn't your environment. I mean land-based civilization. Any time you come above high tide you ought to carry a tag, the way sandhogs do. Something like 'This man is not completely amphibious, and may get into trouble ashore. Rush to nearest salt water and immerse.'"

"I'll buy it," I said. "Only the whole thing started at sea. That can scare you."

"Have you told him yet?" she asked Bill.

"I'm going to right now." He pushed the untouched eggs off his plate onto mine and lighted a cigarette. "Try this on for size—your man was forty-eight to fifty, six feet, a hundred and seventy pounds, brown hair with a little gray in it, brown eyes, mustache, quiet, gentlemanly, closemouthed, and boat-crazy."

"Right," I said. "Except for the mustache."

"Somebody may have told him about razors. He came here about two and a half years ago—February of nineteen-fifty-six, to be exact—and he seemed to have plenty of money. He rented a house on one of the islands—a big, elaborate one with private dock—and bought that sport fisherman, a thirty-foot sloop, and a smaller sailboat of some kind. He was a bachelor, widower, or divorced. He had a Cuban couple who took care of the house and garden, and a man named Charley Grimes to skipper the fishing boat. Apparently didn't work at anything, and spent nearly all his time fishing and sailing. Had several girl friends around town, most of whom would have probably married him if he'd ever asked them, but it appears he never told them any more about himself than he told anybody else. His name was Brian Hardy, and the name of the fishing boat was the *Princess Pat*. You begin to get it now?"

"It all fits," I said excitedly. "Every bit of it. That was Baxter, beyond a doubt."

"That's what I'm afraid of," Bill replied. "Brian Hardy's been dead for over two months. And this is the part you're going to love. He was lost at sea."

It began to come back then. "No!" I said. "No—"

Lorraine patted my hand. "Poor old Rogers. Why don't you get married, so you can stay out of trouble? Or be in it all the time and get used to it."

"Understand," I said, "I'm not prejudiced. Some of my best friends are married. It's just that I wouldn't want my sister to marry a married couple."

"It happened in April, and I think you were somewhere in the out islands," Bill went on. "But you probably heard about it."

"Yeah," I said. "Explosion and fire, wasn't it? Somewhere in the Stream."

"That's right. He was alone. He'd had a fight with Grimes

that morning and fired him, and was taking the *Princess Pat* across to Bimini himself. He'd told somebody he planned to hire a native skipper and mate for a couple of weeks' marlin fishing. It was good weather with hardly any wind, and the Stream was as flat as Biscayne Bay. He left around noon, and should have been over there in three or four hours. Afterward, there were two boats that reported seeing him drifting around, but he didn't ask for help so they didn't go over. Some time after dark he called the Coast Guard—"

"Sure," I broke in. "That was it. I remember now. He was talking to them right at the moment she blew up."

Bill nodded. "It was easy enough to figure out what happened. When he got hold of them, he said he'd been having engine trouble all afternoon. Dirt or rust in the fuel tanks. He'd been blowing out fuel lines and cleaning strainers and settling bowls and probably had the bilges full of gasoline by that time. He'd know enough not to smoke, of course, so it must have been the radio itself that set it off. Maybe a sparking brush on the converter, or a relay contact. That was the Coast Guard theory. Anyway, he went dead right in the middle of a sentence. Then about fifteen minutes later a northbound tanker pretty well out in the Stream off Fort Lauderdale reported what looked like a boat afire over to the eastward of them. They changed course and went over, and got there before the Coast Guard, but there wasn't anything they could do. She was a mass of flame by then and in a matter of minutes she burned to the waterline and sank. The Coast Guard cruised around for several hours, hoping he'd been able to jump, but if he had he'd already drowned. They never found any trace of him. There wasn't any doubt, of course, as to what boat it was. That was just about the position he'd reported. He'd been drifting north in the Stream all the time his engines were conked out."

"Did they ever recover his body?" I asked.

"No."

"Did his life-insurance companies pay off?"

"As far as anybody could ever find out, he didn't carry any life insurance."

We looked at each other in silence. We both nodded.

"When they come after you," Lorraine said, "tell them to wait for me. I think so too."

"Sure," I said excitedly. "Look—that's the very thing that's been puzzling me all the time. I mean, why those three goons were so sure I'd put him ashore somewhere, without even knowing about the letter. It's simply because he'd done it to 'em once before."

"Not so fast," Bill cautioned. "Remember, this happened at least twenty miles offshore. And on his way out that day he stopped at a marine service station in Government Cut and gassed up. They were positive he didn't have a dinghy. Sport fishermen seldom or never do, of course, so they'd have noticed if he had."

"That doesn't prove a thing," I said, "except that we're right. He *wanted* it known he didn't have another boat with him. Somebody else took him off, and five will get you ten it was a girl named Paula Stafford. The Stream was flat; she could have come out from Fort Lauderdale in any kind of power cruiser, or even one of those big, fast outboard jobs. Finding him in the dark might be a tough job for a land-lubber, unless he gave her a portable RDF and a signal from the *Princess Pat* to home on, but actually she wouldn't have to do it in the dark. She could have been already out there before sundown, lying a mile or so away where she wouldn't have any trouble picking up his lights. Or if there were no other boats around, she could have gone alongside before it got dark."

"But neither the tanker nor the Coast Guard saw any other boat when they got there."

"They wouldn't," I said. "Look. They took it for granted the explosion occurred while he was talking to them, because his radio went dead. Well, his radio went dead simply because he turned it off. Then he threw several gallons of gasoline around the cabin and cockpit, rigged a fuse of some kind that would take a few minutes to set it off, got in the other boat, and shoved. It would have taken the tanker possibly ten minutes to get there, even after they spotted the fire. So with a fast boat, Baxter was probably five to seven miles away and running without lights when it showed up, and by the time the Coast Guard arrived he was ashore having a drink in some cocktail lounge in Fort Lauderdale. It would be easy. That's the reason I asked about the insurance. It would be so simple to fake that if he had a really big policy they probably wouldn't pay off until after seven years, or whatever it is."

"Well, he didn't have any," Bill replied, "so that was no strain. He also had no heirs that anybody has been able to locate, and the only estate besides the other boats seems to be a checking account with about eleven thousand in it."

"What else did you find out?" I asked.

"I pulled his package in the morgue, but there wasn't a

great deal in it after the clippings for those first few days. So I started calling people. The police are still trying to locate some of his family. The house is sitting there vacant; he had a lease, and paid the rent on a yearly basis, so it has until next February to run. Nobody can understand his financial setup. The way he lived was geared to a hell of a big income, but they don't know where it came from. They couldn't find any investments of any kind, no stocks, bonds, real estate, savings, or anything. Just the checking account."

"Well, the bank must know how the checking account was maintained."

"Yes. Mostly by big cashiers' checks, ten thousand or more at a time, from out-of-town banks. He could have bought them himself."

"That sounds as if he were on the run, and hiding from somebody, even then. If he had a lot of money it was in cash, and he kept it that way so he could take it with him if he had to disappear."

"The police figure it about the same way. After all, he wouldn't be exactly unique. We get our share of lamsters, absconding bank types, and Latin American statesmen who got out just ahead of the firing squad with a trunk full of loot."

I lighted a cigarette. "I want to get in that house. Do you know the address?"

He nodded. "I know the address, but you couldn't get in. It'd be tough, even for a pro. That's about seventy thousand dollars' worth of house, and in that class they don't make it easy for burglars."

"I've got to! Look—Baxter's going to drive me insane, get

me killed, or land me in jail. There must be an explanation for him. If I could only find out who the hell he really was, I'd at least have a place to start."

He shook his head. "You wouldn't find it there. The police have been over every inch of it, and they found absolutely nothing that would give them a lead, not a letter or a clipping or a scrap of paper, or even anything he'd bought before he came to Miami. They even checked the labels and laundry marks in his clothes, and they're all local. He apparently moved in exactly the way a baby is born—naked, and with no past life whatever."

I nodded. "That's the impression you begin to get after a while. He came aboard the *Topaz* the same way. He just appears, like a revelation."

"But about the house," Bill went on, "I haven't told you everything yet. I was in it this afternoon, and there's just a chance I stumbled onto something. I don't know."

I looked up quickly. "What?"

"Don't get your hopes up. The chances are a thousand to one it's nothing at all. It's only an autographed book and a letter."

"How'd you get in?" I demanded. "What book is it, and who's the letter from?"

He lighted another cigarette. "The police let me in. I went to a lieutenant I know and made him a proposition. I wanted to do a Sunday-supplement sort of piece on Hardy, and if they'd cooperate it might help both of us. Any newspaper publicity is always helpful when you're trying to locate friends or relatives of somebody who's dead. You know." He made an impatient gesture, and went on.

"Anyway, they were agreeable. They had a key to the place, and sent a man with me. We spent about an hour in the house, prowling through all the desks and table drawers and his clothes and leafing through books and so on—all the stuff that had been sifted before. We didn't find anything, of course. But when we were leaving, I noticed some mail on a small table in the front hall. The table was under the mail slot, but we hadn't seen it when we came in because it's behind the door when it's open.

"Apparently what had happened was that this stuff had been delivered between the time the police were there last —shortly after the accident—and the time somebody finally got around to notifying the Post Office he was dead. Anyway, it was all postmarked in April. The detective opened it, but none of it amounted to anything. There were two or three bills and some circulars, and this letter and the book. They were both postmarked Santa Barbara, California, and the letter was from the author of the book. It was just a routine sort of thing, saying the book was being returned, autographed, as he'd requested, and thanking him for his interest. The detective kept them both, of course, but he let me read the letter, and I got another copy of the book out of the public library. Just a minute."

He went into the living room and came back with it. I recognized it immediately; in fact, I had a copy of it aboard the *Orion*. It was an arty and rather expensive job, a collection of some of the most beautiful photographs of sailing craft I'd ever seen. Most of them were racing yachts under full sail, and the title of it was *Music in the Wind*. A good many of the photographs had been taken by the girl who'd collected and edited the job and written the descriptive material. Her name was Patricia Reagan.

"I'm familiar with it," I said, looking at him a little blankly. I couldn't see what he had in mind. "They're beautiful photographs. Hey, you don't mean—"

He shook his head. "No. There's no picture of anyone in here who resembles the description of Brian Hardy. I've already looked."

"Then what is it?" I asked.

"A couple of things," he replied. "And both pretty far out. The first is that he had hundreds of books, but this is the only one that was autographed. The other thing is the name."

"Patricia!" I said.

He nodded. "I checked on it. When he bought that fishing boat its name was *Dolphin III*, or something like that. He was the one who changed it to *Princess Pat*."

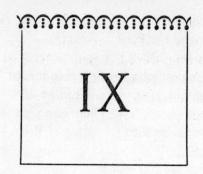

IX

"You both have a boarding-house reach," Lorraine said.

"Where I'm sitting, I need one," I replied. "How was the letter worded? Any indication at all that she knew him?"

"No. Polite, but completely impersonal. Apparently he'd written her, praising the book and sending a copy to be autographed. She signed it and sent it back. Thank you, over, and out. The only possibility is that she might have known him by some other name."

"You don't remember the address?"

He looked pained. "That's a hell of a question to ask a reporter. Here." He fished in his wallet and handed me a slip of paper. On it was scrawled, *"Patricia Reagan, 16 Belvedere Pl., Sta. Brba., Calif."*

I looked at my watch and saw that even with the time difference it would be almost one a.m. in California. "Hell, call her now," Bill said. I went out in the living room, dialed the operator, gave her the name and address, and held on. While she was getting Information in Santa Barbara I wondered what I'd do if somebody woke me up out of a sound sleep from three thousand miles away to ask me if I'd ever heard of Joe Blow the Third. Well, the worst she could do was hang up.

The phone rang three times. Then a girl said sleepily, "Hello?"

"Miss Patricia Reagan?" the operator asked. "Miami is calling."

"Pat, is that you?" the girl said. "What on earth—"

"No," the operator explained. "The call is for Miss—"

I broke in. "Never mind, Operator. I'll talk to anyone there."

"Thank you. Go ahead, please."

"Hello," I said. "I'm trying to locate Miss Reagan."

"Oh, I'm sorry," the girl replied. "She's not here; I'm her roommate. The operator said Miami, so I thought it was Pat that was calling."

"You mean she's in Miami?"

"Yes. That is, Florida. Near Miami."

"Do you know the address?"

"Yes. I had a letter from her yesterday. Just a moment."

I waited. Then she said, "Hello? Here it is. The nearest town seems to be a place called Marathon. Do you know where that is?"

"Yes," I said. "It's down the Keys."

"She's on Spanish Key, and the mailing address is care of W. R. Holland, RFD One."

"Does she have a telephone?"

"I think so. But I don't know the number."

"Is she a guest there?" I didn't like the idea of waking up an entire household with a stupid question.

"She's staying in the house while the owners are in Europe. While she works on some magazine articles. I don't know how well you know her, but I wouldn't advise interrupting her when she's working."

"No," I said. "Only while she's sleeping. And thanks a million."

I hung up. Bill and Lorraine had come into the living room. I told them, and put in the call to the Marathon exchange. The phone rang, and went on ringing. *Five. Six. Seven.* It was a very big house, or she was a sound sleeper.

"Hello." She had a nice voice, but she sounded cross. Well, I thought, who wouldn't?

"Miss Reagan?" I asked.

"Yes. What is it?"

"I want to apologize for waking you up this time of morning, but this is vitally important. It's about a man named Brian Hardy. Did you ever know him?"

"No. I've never heard of him."

"Please think carefully. He used to live in Miami, and he asked you to autograph a copy of *Music in the Wind.* Which, incidentally, is a very beautiful book. I have a copy of it myself."

"Thank you," she said, a little more pleasantly. "Now that you mention it, I do seem to have a hazy recollection of the name. Frankly, I'm not flooded with requests for autographs, and as I recall he mailed the book to me."

"That's right. But as far as you know, you've never met him?"

"No. I'm positive of that. And his letter said nothing about knowing me."

"Was the letter handwritten or typed?"

"Typed, I think. Yes, I'm sure of that."

"I see. Well, did you ever know a man named Wendell Baxter?"

"No. And would you mind telling me just who you are and what this is all about? Are you drunk?"

"I'm not drunk," I said. "I'm in trouble up to my neck, and I'm trying to find somebody who knew this man. I've got a wild hunch that he knew you. Let me describe him."

"All right," she said wearily. "Which shall we take first? Mr. Hardy, or the other one?"

"They're the same man," I said. "He would be about fifty years old, slender, maybe a little over six feet tall, brown eyes, graying brown hair, distinguished looking, and well educated. Have you ever known anybody who would fit that?"

"No." I thought I detected just the slightest hesitancy, but decided I was reaching for it. "Not that I recall. Though it's rather general."

"Try!" I urged her. "Listen. He was a quiet man, very reserved, and courteous. He didn't use glasses, even for reading. He was a heavy smoker. Chesterfields, two or three packs a day. Not particularly dark-complexioned, but he took a good tan. He was a superb small-boat sailor, a natural helmsman, and I would guess he'd done quite a bit of ocean racing. Does any of that remind you of anyone you've ever known?"

"No," she said coldly. "It doesn't."

"Are you sure? No one at all?"

"Well, it does happen to be an excellent description of my father. But if this is a joke of some kind, I must say it's in very poor taste."

"What?"

"My father is dead." The receiver banged in my ear as she hung up.

I dropped the instrument back on the cradle and reached dejectedly for a cigarette. Then I stopped, and stared at Bill. How stupid could I get? Of course he was. That was the one thing in common in all the successive manifestations of Wendell Baxter; each time you finally ran him down, he was certain to be dead.

I grabbed up the phone and put in the call again. After it had rung for three minutes with no answer I gave up.

"Here's your ticket," Bill said. "But I still think you ought to take the car. Or let me drive you down there."

"If they picked me up, you'd be in a jam too. I'll be safe enough on the bus, this far from the Miami terminal."

It was after sunrise now, and we were parked near the bus station in Homestead, about thirty miles south of Miami. I'd shaved and changed into a pair of Bill's slacks and a sport shirt, and was wearing sun glasses.

"Don't get your hopes too high," Bill cautioned. He was worried about me. "It's flimsy as hell. She'd know whether her own father was dead or not."

"I know," I said. "But I've got to talk to her."

"Suppose it's nothing, then what? Call me, and let me come after you."

"No," I said. "I'll call the FBI. I'm not doing myself any good, running like this, and if I keep it up too long Bonner and those other goons may catch up with me."

The bus pulled in. Bill made a gesture with his thumb and forefinger. "Luck, pal."

"Thanks," I said. I slid out of the car, and climbed aboard. The bus was about two-thirds filled, and several passengers were reading copies of the *Herald* with my description on the front page, but no one paid any attention to me. There was no picture, thank God. I found a seat in the rear beside a sailor who'd fallen asleep, and watched Bill drive away.

In a little over an hour we were on Key Largo and beginning the long run down the Overseas Highway. It was a hot June morning with brilliant sunlight and a gentle breeze out of the southeast. I stared out at the water with its hundred gradations of color from bottle green to indigo and wished I could wake up from this dream to find myself back aboard the *Orion* somewhere in the out islands of the Bahamas. How long had it been going on now? This was— what? Monday? Only forty-eight hours. It seemed a month. And all it ever did was get worse. I'd started out with one dead Baxter, and now I had three.

And what would I prove, actually, if I did find out who he was? That wouldn't change anything. It would still be my unsupported word against the rest of the world as to what had become of him and that money he'd said he had. I was beating my brains out for nothing. No matter how you sliced it, there was only one living witness, I was it, and there'd never be any more.

We passed Islamorada and Marathon. It was shortly after eleven when we rolled onto Spanish Key and pulled to a stop in front of the filling station and general store. I got down, feeling the sudden impact of the heat after the air-conditioning, and the bus went on. I could see the secondary road where it emerged from the pines about a quarter of a mile ahead, but I didn't know which branch I wanted. A gaunt, leathery-faced man in overalls and a railroad cap was cleaning the windshield of a car in the station driveway. I called over to him.

"Holland?" He pointed. "Take the road to the left. It's about a mile and a half."

"Thanks," I said.

For the first half mile there were no houses at all. The unsurfaced marl road wound through low pine and palmetto slash that was more like the interior of Florida than the Keys. From time to time I caught glimpses of water off to my right. Then the road swung in that direction and I passed near some beach houses and could see out across the half-mile channel separating Spanish Key from the next one to the westward. The houses were boarded up with hurricane shutters as if their owners were gone for the summer. I stopped to light a cigarette and mop the sweat from my face. All sound of cars passing on the Overseas Highway had died out behind me now. If she wanted an isolated place to work, I thought, she'd found it.

The pine began to thin out a little and the road swung eastward now, paralleling the beach along the south side of the Key. The next mailbox was Holland's. The house was on the beach, about a hundred yards back from the road, with a curving drive and a patch of green lawn in front. It was large for a beach house, solidly constructed of concrete block and stucco, and dazzling white in the sun, with a red tile roof and bright aluminum awnings over the windows and the door. In the carport on the right was an MG with California license plates. She was home.

I went up the short concrete walk and rang the bell. Nothing happened. I pushed the button again, and waited. There was no sound except the lapping of water on the beach around in back, and somewhere farther offshore an outboard motor. About two hundred yards up the beach was another house somewhat similar to this one, but there was no car in evidence and it appeared to be unoccupied. There was still no sound from inside. The drapes were drawn behind the jalousie windows on either side of the door. The outboard motor sounded nearer. I stepped around the corner and saw it. It was coming this way, a twelve- or fourteen-foot runabout planing along at a good clip. At the wheel was a girl in a brief splash of yellow bathing suit.

There was a long low porch back here, another narrow strip of lawn, a few coconut palms leaning seaward, and a glaring expanse of white coral sand along the shore. There were several pieces of brightly colored lawn furniture on the porch and under the palms, and a striped umbrella and some beach pads out on the sand. The water was very shoal, and there was no surf because of the reefs offshore and the fact that the breeze had almost died out now. Far out I could see a westbound tanker skirting the inshore edge of the Stream. A wooden pier ran out into the water about fifty feet, and the girl was coming alongside it now. I started out to take a line for her, but she beat me there. She lifted out a mask and snorkel and an under-water camera in a clear plastic housing, and stepped onto the pier.

She was slender and rather tall, a girl with a deep tan and dark wine-red hair. Her back was toward me momentarily as she made the painter fast. She straightened and turned then, and I saw her eyes were brown. The face was slender, with a very nice mouth and a stubborn chin, and was as smoothly tanned as the rest of her. There was no really striking resemblance to Baxter, but she could very well be his daughter.

"Good morning," I said. "Miss Reagan?"

She nodded coolly. "Yes. What is it?"

"My name is Stuart Rogers. I'd like to talk to you for a minute."

"You're the man who called me this morning." It was a statement, rather than a question.

"Yes," I said, just as bluntly. "I want to ask you about your father."

"Why?"

"Why don't we go over in the shade and sit down?" I suggested.

"All right." She reached for the camera. I picked it up and followed her. She was about five feet eight inches tall, I thought. Her hair was wet at the ends, as if the bathing cap hadn't covered it completely, and tendrils of it stuck to the nape of her neck. It was a little cooler on the porch. She sat down on a chaise with one long smooth leg doubled under her, and looked up questioningly at me. I held out cigarettes, and she thanked me and took one. I lighted it for her.

I sat down across from her. "This won't take long. I'm not prying into your personal affairs just because I haven't got anything better to do. You said your father was dead. Could you tell me when he died?"

"In nineteen-fifty-six," she replied.

Hardy had showed up in Miami in February of 1956. That didn't allow much leeway. "What month?" I asked.

"January," she said.

I sighed. We were over that one.

The brown eyes began to burn. "Unless you have some good explanation for this, Mr. Rogers—"

"I do. I have a very good one. However, you can get rid of me once and for all by answering just one more question. Were you present at his funeral?"

She gasped. "Why did you ask that?"

"I think you know by now," I said. "There wasn't any funeral, was there?"

"No." She leaned forward tensely. "What are you trying to say? That you think he's still alive?"

"No," I said. "I'm sorry. He is dead now. He died of a heart attack on the fifth of this month aboard my boat in the Caribbean."

Her face was pale under the tan, and I was afraid she was going to faint. She didn't, however. She shook her head. "No. It's impossible. It was somebody else—"

"What happened in nineteen-fifty-six?" I asked. "And where?"

"It was in Arizona. He went off into the desert on a hunting trip, and got lost."

"Arizona? What was he doing there?"

"He lived there," she replied. "In Phoenix."

I wondered if I'd missed, after all, when I'd been so near. That couldn't be Baxter. He was a yachtsman, a seaman; you couldn't even imagine him in a desert environment. Then I remembered *Music in the Wind.* She hadn't acquired that intense feeling for the beauty of sail by watching somebody's colored slides. "He wasn't a native?" I said.

"No. We're from Massachusetts. He moved to Phoenix in nineteen-fifty."

Now we were getting somewhere. "Look, Miss Reagan," I said, "you admitted the description I gave you over the phone could be that of your father. You also admit you have no definite proof he's dead; he merely disappeared. Then why do you refuse to believe he could be the man I'm talking about?"

"I should think it would be obvious," she replied curtly. "My father's name was Clifford Reagan. Not Hardy—or whatever it was you said."

"He could have changed it."

"And why would he?" The brown eyes blazed again, but I had a feeling there was something defensive about her anger.

"I don't know," I said.

"There are several other reasons," she went on. "He couldn't have lived in that desert more than two days without water. The search wasn't called off until long after everybody had given up all hope he could still be alive. It's been two and a half years. If he'd found his way out, don't you consider it at least a possibility he might have let me know?

Or do you think the man who died on your boat was suffering from amnesia and didn't know who he was?"

"No," I said. "He knew who he was, all right."

"Then I believe we've settled the matter," she said, starting to get up. "It wasn't my father. So if you'll excuse me—"

"Not so fast," I snapped. "I'm already in about all the trouble one man can get in, and you can't make it any worse by calling the police and having me thrown in jail. So don't try to brush me off till we're finished, because that's the only way you're going to do it. I think you'd better tell me how he got lost."

For a moment I wouldn't have offered much in the way of odds that she wasn't going to slap me across the face. She was a very proud girl with a lot of spirit. Then she appeared to get her temper in hand. "All right," she said.

"He was hunting quail," she went on. "In some very hilly and inaccessible desert country ninety or a hundred miles southwest of Tucson. He'd gone alone. That was Saturday morning, and he wasn't really missed until he failed to show up at the bank on Monday."

"Didn't you or your mother know where he was?" I asked.

"He and my mother were divorced in nineteen-fifty," she replied. "At the same time he moved to Phoenix. We were living in Massachusetts. He had remarried, but was separated from his second wife."

"Oh," I said. "I'm sorry. Go on."

"The bank called his apartment, thinking he might be ill. When they could get no answer, they called the apartment-house manager. He said he'd seen my father leave on Saturday with his gun and hunting clothes, but he wasn't sure where he'd planned to hunt or how long he intended to stay. The sheriff's office was notified, and they located the sporting-goods store where he'd bought some shells Friday afternoon. He'd told the clerk the general locality he was going to hunt in. They organized a search party, but it was such an immense area and so rough and remote that it was Wednesday before they even found the car. It was near an old trace of a road at least twenty miles from the nearest ranch house. He'd apparently got lost while he was hunting and couldn't find his way back to it. They went on searching with jeeps and horses and even planes until the following Sunday, but they never did find him. Almost a year later some uranium prospectors found his hunting coat; it was six or seven miles from where the car had been. Are you satisfied now?"

"Yes," I said. "But not quite the way you think. Have you read the paper this morning?"

She shook her head. "It's still in the mailbox. I haven't gone after it yet."

"I'll bring it," I said. "I want you to read something."

I went and got it. "I'm the Captain Rogers referred to," I said as I handed it to her. "The man who signed himself Brian in the letter is the same one who told me his name was Wendell Baxter."

She read it through. Then she folded the paper and put it aside defiantly. "It's absurd," she said. "It's been two and a half years. And my father never had twenty-three thousand dollars. Nor any reason for calling himself Brian."

"Listen," I told her. "One month after your father disappeared in that desert a man who could be his double arrived in Miami, rented a big home on an island in Biscayne Bay, bought a forty-thousand-dollar sport fisherman he renamed the *Princess Pat*—"

She gasped.

I went on relentlessly. "—and lived there like an Indian prince with no apparent source of income until the night of April seventh of this year, when *he* disappeared. He was lost at sea when the *Princess Pat* exploded, burned to the waterline, and sank, twenty miles off the Florida coast at Fort Lauderdale. And again, no body was ever found. His name was Brian Hardy, and he was the one who sent you that book to be autographed. Slightly less than two months later, on May thirty-first, Brian Hardy came aboard my ketch in Cristobal, using the name of Wendell Baxter. I'm not guessing here, or using descriptions, because I saw a photograph of Hardy, and this was the same man. And I say Hardy was your father. Do you have any kind of photograph or snapshot?"

She gave a dazed shake of the head. "Not here. I have some in the apartment in Santa Barbara."

"Do you agree now it was your father?"

"I don't know. The whole thing is so utterly pointless. Why would he do it?"

"He was running from somebody," I said. "In Arizona, and then in Miami, and again in Panama."

"But from whom?"

"I don't know," I said. "I was hoping you might. But the thing I really want to know is this—did your father ever have a heart attack?"

"No," she said. "Not that I ever heard."

"Is there any history of heart or coronary disease in the family at all?"

She shook her head. "I don't think so."

I lighted a cigarette and stared out across the sun-drenched blues and greens over the reefs. I was doing just beautifully. Apparently all I'd accomplished so far was to establish that aboard the *Topaz* Baxter had died for the third time with great finality and dramatic effect without leaving a body around to prove it. So all I had to do was convince everybody that this time it was for real. If he died of bubonic plague on the speaker's platform at an AMA convention, I thought bitterly, and was cremated in Macy's window, nobody would take it seriously. He'll turn up fellas; just you wait.

"Does the name Slidell mean anything to you?" I asked.

"No," she said. I was convinced she was telling the truth. "I've never heard it before."

"Do you know where he could have got that money?"

She ran despairing hands through her hair, and stood up. "No. Mr. Rogers, none of this makes the slightest sense to me. It *couldn't* have been my father."

"But you know it was, don't you?" I said.

She nodded. "I'm afraid so."

"Did you say he worked for a bank?"

"Yes. In the Trust Department of the Drovers National."

"There was no shortage in his accounts?"

For an instant I thought the anger was going to flare again. Then she said wearily, "No. Not this time."

"This time?"

She made a little gesture of resignation. "Since he may be

the one who got you into this trouble, I suppose you have a right to know. He did take some money once, from another bank. I don't see how it could have any bearing on this, but maybe it has. If you'll wait while I shower and change, I'll tell you about it."

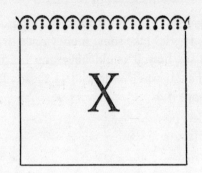

X

SHE brushed sand from her bare feet and opened the door at the left end of the porch. The kitchen was bright with colored tile and white enamel. I followed her through an arched doorway into a large dining and living room. "Please sit down," she said. "I won't be long." She disappeared down a hallway to the right.

I lighted a cigarette and looked around at the room. It was comfortable, and the light pleasantly subdued after the glare of the white coral sand outside. The drapes over the front window were of some loosely woven dark green material, and the lighter green walls and bare terrazzo floor added to the impression of coolness. Set in the wall to the left, next to the carport, was an air-conditioner unit whose faint humming made the only sound. Above it was a mounted permit, a very large one. Between it and the front window on that side was a hi-fi set in a blond cabinet. At the rear of the room was a sideboard, and a dining table made of bamboo and heavy glass. A long couch and two armchairs with a teak coffee table between them formed a conversational group near the center of the room. The couch and chairs were bamboo with brightly colored cushions. On the other side of the room, between the hallway and the front, were stacks of loaded book shelves. Just to the right of the hallway was a massive desk on which were a telephone, a portable typewriter, several boxes of paper, and two more cameras, a Rolleiflex and a 35-mm job. I walked over to the desk and saw that it also held several trays of colored slides and a pile of photographs of Keys scenes, mostly eight-by-ten blowups in both black-and-white and color. I wondered if she'd done them, and then remembered *Music in the Wind*. She was an artist with a camera. Somewhere down the hall was the muted sound of a shower running.

In a few minutes she came back. She had changed to a crisp summery dress of some pale blue material, and was bare-legged and wearing sandals. Her hair, cut rather short in a careless, pixie effect, seemed a little darker than it had in the sun. Patricia Reagan was a very attractive girl. She had regained her composure somewhat, and managed a smile. "I'm sorry to keep you waiting."

"Not at all," I said. We sat down and lighted cigarettes.

"How did you locate me?" she asked.

I told her. "Your roommate in Santa Barbara said you were doing some magazine articles."

She made a deprecating gesture. "Not on assignment, I'm afraid. I'm not a professional yet. An editor has promised to look at an article on the Keys, and I had a chance to stay in this house while Mr. and Mrs. Holland are in

Europe. They were neighbors of ours in Massachusetts. And in the meantime I'm doing some colored slides, under-water shots along the reefs."

"Skin-diving alone's not a very good practice," I said.

"Oh, I'm just working in shallow water. But the whole area's fascinating, and the water's beautiful."

I grinned. "I'm a Floridian, and I don't like to sound unpatriotic, but you ought to try the Bahamas. The colors of the water under the right light conditions almost make you hurt."

She nodded somberly. "I was there once, when I was twelve. My mother and father and I cruised in the Exumas and around Eleuthera for about a month in a shallow-draft yawl."

"A charter?" I asked.

"No. It was ours. He and I brought it down, and Mother flew to Nassau to join us. She always got sick offshore."

"What was the name of the yawl?"

The brown eyes met mine in a quick glance. Then she shook her head, a little embarrassed. "*Enchantress.* Princess Pat was a pet name, one of those top-secret jokes between fathers and very young daughters. He was the only one who ever used it."

"I'm sorry about all this," I said. "But how did he get to Phoenix?"

Downhill, as it turned out. She told me, and even after all this time there was hurt and bewilderment in it. The Reagans were from a small town named Elliston on the coast of Massachussetts near Lynn. They'd always been sailors, either professional or amateur, several having been mates and shipmasters during the clipper-ship era in the 1840s and 50s and another a privateer during the Revolution. Clifford Reagan belonged to the yacht club and had sailed in a number of ocean races, though not in his own boat.

I gathered his father was fairly well-to-do, though she made as little of this as possible. He'd been in the foundry business and in real estate, and owned considerable stock in the town's leading bank and was on its board of directors. Clifford Reagan went to work in the bank when he finished college. He married a local girl, and Patricia was their only child. You could tell she and her father were very close when she was small. Then when she was sixteen the whole thing went on the rocks.

Her mother and father were divorced, but that was only the beginning. When her mother's attorneys wanted an accounting of the community property the rest of it was discovered; he'd lost not only everything they owned gambling on Canadian mining stocks, but also $17,000 he'd taken from the bank.

"Nobody ever knew about it except the president of the bank and the family," she said, staring down at her hands in her lap. "My grandfather made the shortage good, so he wasn't prosecuted. The only stipulation was that he resign, and never work in a bank again."

"But he was working in one in Phoenix," I said.

She nodded. "Actually, there was no way anyone could stop him. It had all been so hushed up before that even the bonding company didn't know about it. Grandfather was afraid it would happen again, but what could he do? Tell

the bank out there that his own son had stolen money?
And perhaps ruin the last chance he'd ever have to live it
down and redeem himself?"

"But how did a man who was already past forty get a job
in a bank without references?" I asked.

"A woman," she said. "His second wife."

Reagan had probably settled on Arizona as being about
as remote from any connection with his past life as it would
be possible to get and still stay on the same planet. He'd
worked for a while as an account representative in a broker-
age office, and soon came to know a great many people in
some of the high-bracket suburbs of Phoenix. He met Mrs.
Canning about that time, and married her in 1951. She was
the widow of a Columbus, Ohio, real-estate developer who
had bought a big ranch near Phoenix and raised quarter
horses. She also owned a big block of stock in the Drovers
National, so nothing could be simpler than Reagan's going
to work there if that was what he wanted to do.

The marriage didn't last—they were separated in 1954—
but oddly enough the job did. They liked him at the bank,
and he worked at the job and was good at it. The distinguished appearance, quiet, well-bred manner, and the fact
that he was on good terms with lots of wealthy potential
customers did him no harm either. He was promoted several
times, and by 1956 was in charge of the trust department.

"He was unhappy, though," she went on. "I think des-
perately unhappy. I could sense it, even though we couldn't
talk to each other the way we used to. I saw him only once
a year, when I went out there for two weeks after school
was out. We both tried very hard, but I guess it's a special

kind of country that fathers and very young daughters live
in, and once you leave it you can never go back. We'd play
golf, and go riding, and skeet shooting, and he'd take me to
parties, but the real lines of communication were down."

She realized that he hated the desert. He was in the
wrong world, and he was too old now to go somewhere else
and start over. She didn't think he drank much; he simply
wasn't the type for it. But she thought there were lots of
girls, each one probably progressively younger, and trips to
Las Vegas, even though he would have to be careful about
that in the banking business.

She was a senior in college that January in 1956 when
the call came from the sheriff's office. She flew out to
Phoenix. "I was afraid," she went on, "and so was Grandfather. Neither of us believed they'd ever find him alive.
Suicide was in our minds, though for different reasons.
Grandfather was afraid he'd got in trouble again. That he'd
taken money from the bank."

"But he hadn't?" I asked.

"No," she said. "Naturally, it would have been discovered if he had. He even had several hundred dollars in his
own account, and almost a month's salary due him."

There you are, I thought; it was an absolutely blank wall.
He hadn't stolen from the bank, but he'd deliberately dis-
appeared. And when he showed up a month later as Brian
Hardy he was rich.

She had fallen silent. I lighted a cigarette. Well, this must
be the end of the line; I might as well call the FBI. Then
she said quietly, "Would you tell me about it?"

I told her, playing down the pain of the heart attack and

making it as easy for her as I could. I explained about the
split mains'l and being becalmed, and the fact that I had
no choice but to bury him at sea. Without actually lying
about it, I managed to gloss over the sketchy aspect of the
funeral and the fact that I hadn't known all the sea-burial
service. I told her it was Sunday, and gave the position, and
tried to tell her what kind of day it was. She gave a little
choked cry and turned her face away, and I looked down
at my cigarette when she got up abruptly and went out in
the kitchen. I sat there feeling rotten. Even with all the
trouble he'd got me into, I'd liked him, and I was beginning
to like her.

Well, I'd known all along it wasn't going to be easy when
I had to face his family and tell them about it. And it was
even worse now because, while she knew in her heart that
it was her father, there could never be any final proof. That
little residue of doubt would always remain, along with all
the unanswerable questions. Was he lying somewhere out
in the desert, or under two miles of water in the Caribbean
Sea? And wherever he was, *why* was he there? What had
happened? What was he running from?

Then suddenly it was back again, that strange feeling of
uneasiness that always came over me when I remembered
the moment of his burial, that exact instant in which I'd
stood at the rail and watched his body slide into the depths.
There was no explanation for it. I didn't even know what
it was. When I reached for it, it was gone, like a bad dream
only partly remembered, and all that was left was this form-
less dread that something terrible was going to happen, or
already had. I tried to shrug it off. Maybe it *had* been a

premonition. Why keep worrying about it now? I'd already got all the bad news.

She came back in a minute, and if she'd been crying she had carefully erased the evidence. She was carrying two bottles of Coke from the refrigerator. "What are you going to do now?" she asked.

"I don't know," I said. "Call the FBI, I suppose. I'd rather try convincing them than those gorillas. Oh. I suppose this is pretty hopeless, but did you ever hear of a man called Bonner? J. R. Bonner?" The name would be phony, of course. I described him.

She shook her head. "No. I'm sorry."

"I hate to drag you into this," I said, "but I'll have to tell them. There'll probably be an investigation of your father."

"It can't be helped," she said.

I lighted a cigarette. "You're the only one so far who hasn't accused me of killing him, stealing his money, or putting him ashore and lying about his death. Don't you think I did, or are you just being polite?"

She gave me a brief smile. "I don't believe you did. It's just occurred to me that I know you—at least by reputation. Some friends of mine in Lynn speak very highly of you."

"Who?" I asked.

"Ted and Frances Holt. They've sailed with you two or three times."

"For the past three years," I said. "They've shot some terrific under-water movies around the Exumas."

"I suppose one of us really ought to say it's a small world," she mused. "Mr. Rogers—"

"Stuart," I said.

"Stuart. Why doesn't anybody seem to think this man Keefer could have taken all that money—assuming it was even aboard? He seems to have had a sizable amount nobody can explain."

"They'd have found it," I said. "When they add up what was in the hotel safe and what he conceivably spent, it still comes out to less than four thousand, and not even a drunk could throw away nineteen thousand dollars in three days. But the big factor is that he couldn't have had it with him when he left the boat. I was right there. He didn't have any luggage, you see, because all his gear was still on that ship he'd missed in Panama. He'd bought a couple of pairs of dungarees for the trip, but I was standing right beside him when he rolled those up, and he didn't put anything in them. And he didn't have a coat. He might have stowed four thousand dollars in his wallet and in the pockets of his slacks, but not twenty-three thousand, unless it was in very large bills. Which I doubt. A man running and trying to hide out would attract a lot of attention trying to break anything larger than hundreds."

"Maybe he took it ashore when you first docked."

"No. I was with him then too."

She frowned. "Then it must still be aboard the *Topaz*."

"No," I said. "It's been searched twice. By experts."

"Then that seems to leave only one other possibility," she said. She paused, and then went on unhappily. "This isn't easy to say, under the circumstances, but do you suppose he could have been—unbalanced?"

"I don't think so," I said. "I did when I first read the letter, of course. I mean, he said he had twenty-three thousand with him, but nobody else ever saw it. He said he was going to ask me to put him ashore, but he never did. And the fact that he was going to wait and put a wild proposition like that to me *after* we got to sea didn't sound very logical, either. A rational man would have realized how slim the chances were that anybody would go for it, and would have sounded me out before we sailed. But if you look at all these things again, you're not so sure.

"He apparently did have some money with him. Four thousand, anyway. So if he had that much, maybe he had it all. And waiting till we got to sea to proposition me makes sense if you look at it correctly. If he brought it up before we sailed, I might refuse to take him at all. Getting out of the Canal Zone before this Slidell caught up with him was the number-one item. If he brought up the other thing later and I turned him down, at least he was out of Panama and safe for the moment."

"So we wind up right where we started."

"That's right," I said. "With the same two questions. What became of the rest of the money? And why did he change his mind?"

The doorbell chimed.

We exchanged a quick glance, and got to our feet. There'd been no sound of a car outside, nor of footsteps on the walk. She motioned me toward the hallway and started to the door, but before she got there it swung open and a tall man in a gray suit and dark green glasses stepped inside and curtly motioned her back. At the same instant I heard the back door open. I whirled. Standing in the arched doorway to the kitchen was a heavy-shouldered tourist wearing a loud sport shirt, straw cap, and an identical pair of green sun glasses. He removed the glasses and grinned coldly at me. It was Bonner.

Escape was impossible. The first man had a gun; I could see the sagging weight of it in his coat pocket. Patricia gasped, and retreated from him, her eyes wide with alarm. She came back against the desk beside the entrance to the hall. Bonner and the other man came toward me. The latter took out a pack of cigarettes. "We've been waiting for you, Rogers," he said, and held them out toward me. "Smoke?"

For an instant all three of us seemed frozen there, the two of them in an attitude almost of amusement while I looked futilely around for a weapon of some kind and waited dry-mouthed for one of them to move. Then I saw what she was doing, and was more scared than ever. She couldn't get away with it, not with these people, but there was no way I could stop her. The telephone was directly behind her. She had reached back, lifted off the receiver, set it gently on the desk top, and was trying to dial Operator. I picked up one of the Coke bottles. That kept their eyes on me for another second or two. Then the dial clicked.

Bonner swung around, casually replaced the receiver, and chopped his open right hand against the side of her face. It made a sharp, cracking sound in the stillness, like a rifle shot, and she spun around and sprawled on the floor in a confused welter of skirt and slip and long bare legs. I was on him by then, swinging the Coke bottle. It hit him a glancing blow and knocked the straw cap off. He straightened, and I swung it again. He took this one on his forearm and smashed a fist into my stomach.

It tore the breath out of me, but I managed to stay on my feet. I lashed out at his face with the bottle. He drew back his head just enough to let it slide harmlessly past his jaw, grinned contemptuously, and slipped a blackjack from his pocket. He was an artist with it, like a good surgeon with a scalpel. Three swings of it reduced my left arm to a numb and dangling weight; another tore loose a flap of skin on my forehead, filling my eyes with blood. I tried to clinch with him. He pushed me back, dropped the sap, and slammed a short brutal right against my jaw. I fell back against the controls of the air-conditioner unit and slid to the floor. Patricia Reagan screamed. I brushed blood from my face and tried to get up, and for an instant I saw the other man. He didn't even bother to watch. He was half-sitting on the corner of the desk, idly swinging his sun glasses by one curved frame while he looked at some of her photographs.

I made it to my feet and hit Bonner once. That was the last time I was in the fight. He knocked me back against the wall and I fell again. He hauled me up and held me against it with his left while he smashed the right into my face. It was like being pounded with a concrete block. I felt teeth loosen. The room began to wheel before my eyes. Just before it turned black altogether, he dropped me. I tried to get up, and made it as far as my knees. He put his shoe in my face and pushed. I fell back on the floor, gasping for breath, with blood in my mouth and eyes. He looked down at me. "That's for Tampa, sucker."

The other man tossed the photographs back on the desk and stood up. "That'll do," he said crisply. "Put him in that chair."

Bonner hauled me across the floor by one arm and heaved me up into one of the bamboo armchairs in the center of the room. Somebody threw a towel that hit me in the face. I mopped at the blood, trying not to be sick.

"All right," the other man said, "go back to the motel and get Flowers. Then get the car out of sight. Over there in the trees somewhere."

Patricia Reagan was sitting up. Bonner jerked his head toward her. "What about the girl?"

"She stays till we get through."

"Why? She'll just be in the way."

"Use your head. Rogers has friends in Miami, and some of them may know where he is. When he doesn't come back they may call up here looking for him. Put her on the sofa."

Bonner jerked a thumb. "Park it, kid."

She stared at him with contempt.

He shrugged, hauled her up by one arm, and shoved. She shot backward past the end of the coffee table and fell on the sofa across from me. Bonner went out.

"I'm sorry," I said. "It's my fault. But I thought I'd lost them."

"You did, temporarily," the man put in. "But we didn't follow you here. We were waiting for you."

I stared at him blankly.

He pulled the other chair around to the end of the coffee table and sat down where he could watch us both. If Bonner was a journeyman in the field of professional deadliness, this one was a top-drawer executive. It was too evident in the crisp, incisive manner, the stamp of intelligence on the face, and the pitiless, unwavering stare. He could have been anywhere between forty and fifty, and had short, wiry red hair, steel-gray eyes, and a lean face that was coppery with fresh sunburn.

"She doesn't know anything about this," I said.

"We're aware of that, but we weren't sure you were. When we lost you in Tampa we watched for you here, among other places."

Blood continued to drip off my face onto my shirt. I mopped at it with the towel. My eyes were beginning to close and my whole face felt swollen. Talking was difficult through the cut and puffy lips. I wondered how long Bonner would be gone. At the moment I was badly beaten, too weak and sick to get out of the chair, but with a few minutes' rest I might be able to take this one, or at least hold him long enough for her to get away. Then, as if he'd read my thoughts, he lifted the gun from his pocket and shook his head.

"Don't move, Rogers," he said. "You're too valuable to kill, but you wouldn't get far without a knee."

The room fell silent except for the humming of the air-conditioner. Patricia's face was pale, but she forced herself to reach out on the coffee table for a cigarette and light it, and look at him without wavering.

"You can't get away with this," she said.

"Don't be stupid, Miss Reagan," he replied. "We know all about your working habits; nobody comes out here to bother you. You won't even have any telephone calls unless it's somebody looking for Rogers. In which case you'll say he's been here and gone."

She glared defiantly. "And if I don't?"

"You will. Believe me."

"You're Slidell?" I said.

He nodded. "You can call me that."

"Why were you after Reagan?"

"We're still after him," he corrected. "Reagan stole a half million dollars in bonds from me and some other men. We want it back, or what's left of it."

"And I suppose you stole them in the first place?"

He shrugged. "You might say they were a little hot. They were negotiable, of course, but an amount that size is unwieldy; fencing them through the usual channels would entail either a lot of time or a large discount. I met Reagan in Las Vegas, and when I found out what he did I sounded him out; he was just the connection we needed. He didn't want to do it at first, but I found out he owed money to some gamblers in Phoenix and arranged for a little pressure. He came through then. He disposed of a hundred thousand dollars' worth for the commission we agreed on, and we turned the rest of them over to him. I suppose she's told you what happened?"

I nodded.

He went on. "We were keeping a close watch on him, of course, and even when he started out on the hunting trip that Saturday morning we followed him long enough to be sure he wasn't trying to skip out. But he was smarter than we thought. He either had another car hidden out there somewhere, or somebody picked him up. It took us two years to run him down, even with private detectives watching for him in all the likely spots. He was in Miami, but staying out of the night clubs and the big flashy places on the Beach. It was just luck we located him at all. Somebody spotted a picture in a hunting and fishing magazine that seemed to resemble him, and when we ran down the photographer and had a blowup made from the original negative, there was Reagan.

"But he beat us again. He apparently saw the picture too, and when we got to Miami and tracked him down we found he'd been killed two weeks before when his boat exploded and burned between Florida and the Bahamas. At first we weren't too sure this was a fake, but when we searched the house and grounds and couldn't turn up even a safe-deposit key, we began checking his girl friends and found one who'd left for Switzerland the very same day. Or so she'd told everybody. But she was careless. When we searched her apartment we found a travel-agency slip in her wastebasket confirming reservations for a Mr. and Mrs. Charles Wayne on a flight to San Juan. He must have seen us there, because by the time we located him he was gone again. We trailed him to New York. By this time they'd separated and he'd hidden her somewhere because he knew we were closing in on him. He flew to Panama. I was one day behind him then, and missed him by only twelve hours in Cristobal when he left with you."

"And now he's dead," I said.

He smiled coldly. "For the third time."

"I tell you—" I broke off. What was the use? Then I thought of something. "Look, he must have cached the money somewhere."

"Obviously. All except the twenty-three thousand he was using to get away."

"Then you're out of luck. Don't you see that? You know where she is; she's in the hospital in Southport, and if she lives, the police are going to get the whole story out of her. She'll have to tell them where it is."

"She may not know."

"Do you know why she came to Southport?" I said. "She wanted to see me, because she hadn't heard from him. Don't you see I'm telling the truth? If he were still alive he'd have written her."

"Yes. Unless he was running out on her too."

I slumped back in the chair. It was hopeless. And even if I could convince them I was telling the truth, what good was it now? They'd kill us anyway.

"However," he went on, "there is one serious flaw in that surmise. If he'd intended to run out on her, there would have been no point in writing her that letter from Cristobal."

"Then you'll admit he might be dead?"

"That's right. There are a number of very strange angles to this thing, Rogers, but we're going to get to the bottom of them in the next few hours. He could be dead for any one of a number of reasons. You and Keefer could have killed him."

"Oh, for God's sake—"

"You're a dead duck. Your story smelled to begin with, and it gets worse every time you turn it over. Let's take that beautiful report you turned in to the US marshal's office, describing the heart attack. That fooled everybody at first, but if I've found out how you did it, don't you suppose the FBI will too? They may not pay as much for information as I do, but they've got more personnel. You made it sound so convincing. I mean, the average layman trying to make up a heart attack on paper would have been inclined to hoke it up and overplay it a little and say Reagan was doing something very strenuous when it happened, because everybody knows that's always what kills the man with coronary trouble. Everybody, that is, except the medics. They know you can also die of an attack while you're lying in bed waiting for somebody to peel you a grape. And it turns out you know that too. One of your uncles died of a coronary thrombosis when you were about fifteen—"

"I wasn't even present," I said. "It happened in his office in Norfolk, Virginia."

"I know. But you *were* present when he had a previous attack. About a year before, when you and he and your father were fishing on a charter boat off Miami Beach. And he wasn't fighting a fish when it happened. He was just sitting in the fishing chair drinking a bottle of beer. It all adds up, Rogers. It all adds up."

It was the first time I'd even thought of it for years. I started to say so, but I happened to turn then and glance at Patricia Reagan. Her eyes were on my face, and there was doubt in them, and something else that was very close to horror. Under the circumstances, I thought, who could blame her? Then the front door opened. Bonner came in, followed by a popeyed little man carrying a black metal case about the size of a portable tape recorder.

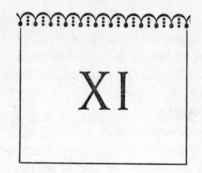

XI

"Both of you stay where you are," Slidell ordered. He stood up and turned to Bonner. "Bring Flowers a table and a chair."

Bonner went down the hall and came back with a small night table. He set it and one of the dining chairs near the chair I was in, and swung me around so I was facing the front window with the table on my right. Then he lighted a cigarette and leaned against the front door, boredly watching.

"This jazz is a waste of time, if you ask me," he remarked.

"I didn't," Slidell said shortly.

Bonner shrugged. I glanced around at Patricia Reagan, but she avoided my eyes and was staring past me at Flowers, as mystified as I was. He was a slightly built little man in his thirties with a bald spot and a sour, pinched face that was made almost grotesque by the slightly bulging eyes. He set the black case on the table and removed the lid. The top panel held a number of controls and switches, but a good part of it was taken up by a window under which was a sheet of graph paper and three styli mounted on little arms.

I glanced up to find Slidell's eyes on me in chill amusement. "We are about to arrive at that universal goal of all the great philosophers, Rogers. Truth."

"What do you mean?"

"That's a lie-detector."

"Cut it out. Where the hell would you get one?"

"There is nothing esoteric about a lie-detector. Almost anybody could make one. Operating it, however, is something else, and that's where we're very fortunate. Flowers is a genius. It talks to him."

Flowers paid no attention. He ran a long cord over to an electrical outlet, and turned the machine on. Then he began connecting it to me as calmly and methodically as if this were a police station. If it occurred to him at all that there was any quality of madness in the situation, he apparently dismissed it as irrelevant. The whole thing was merely a technical problem. He wrapped a blood-pressure cuff about my right arm above the elbow and pumped it up. Then a tube went about my chest. He threw another switch, and the paper began to move. The styli made little jagged lines as they registered my pulse, blood pressure, and respiration. The room became very quiet. He made minor adjustments to the controls, pulled up the chair and sat down, hunched over the thing with the dedicated expression of a priest. He nodded to Slidell.

"All right, Rogers," Slidell said. "All you have to do is answer the questions I put to you. Answer any way you like, but answer. Refuse, and you get the gun barrel across your face."

"Go ahead," I said. It did no good now to think how stupid I'd been not to think of this myself. I could have asked the FBI to give me a lie-detector test.

"It won't work," Bonner said disgustedly. "Everybody knows how they operate. The blood pressure and pulse change when you're upset or scared. So how're you going to tell anything with a meatball that's scared stiff to begin with?"

"There will still be a deviation from the norm," Flowers said contemptuously.

"To translate," Slidell said, "what Flowers means is that if Rogers is scared stiff as a normal condition, the instrument will tell us when he's scared rigid. Now shut up."

Bonner subsided.

"What is your name?" Slidell asked.

"Stuart Rogers."

"Where were you born?"

"Coral Gables, Florida."

"Where did you go to school?"

"The University of Miami."

"What business is your father in?"

"He was an attorney."

"You mean he's dead?"

"Yes," I said.

"What did he die of?"

"He was killed in an automobile accident."

There were fifteen or twenty more of these establishing questions while Flowers intently studied his graphs. Then

Slidell said, "Did you know a man who told you his name was Wendell Baxter?"

"Yes," I said.

"And he sailed with you from Cristobal on June first aboard your boat?"

"Yes."

"And you put him ashore somewhere in Central America or Mexico?"

"No," I said.

Slidell was leaning over Flowers' shoulder, watching the styli. Flowers gave a faint shake of the head. Slidell frowned at me.

"Where *did* you put him ashore?"

"I didn't," I said.

"Where is he?"

"He's dead."

Flowers looked up at Slidell and spread his hands.

"You don't see any change in pattern at all?" Slidell asked.

"No. Of course, it's impossible to tell much with one short record—"

Bonner came over. "I told you it wouldn't work. Let me show you how to get the truth." His hand exploded against the side of my face and rocked me back in the chair. I tasted blood.

"You'll have to keep this fool away from him," Flowers said bitterly. "Look what he's done."

The styli were swinging violently.

"Hate," Flowers explained.

I rubbed my face and stared at Bonner. "Tell your machine it can say that again."

"Get away from him," Slidell ordered.

"Let me have that gun, and give me five minutes—"

"Certainly," Slidell said coldly. "So you can kill him before we find out anything, the way you did Keefer. Can't you get it through your head that Rogers is the last? He's the only person on earth who can answer these questions."

"Well, what good is that if he keeps lying?"

"I'm not sure he is. Reagan could be dead this time. I've told you that before. Now get back."

Bonner moved back to the door. Slidell and Flowers watched while the styli settled down. Patricia Reagan had turned away with her face down on her arms across the back of the couch. I couldn't tell whether she was crying.

"Listen, Rogers," Slidell said, "we're going to get the truth of what happened out there on that boat if it takes a week, and you have to account for every hour of the trip, minute by minute, and we repeat these questions until you crack up and start screaming. The police will never find you, and you can't get away. Do you understand?"

"Yes," I said wearily.

"Good. Is Reagan dead?"

"Yes."

"When did he die?"

"Four days out of Cristobal. On June fifth, at about three-thirty p.m."

"Did you and Keefer kill him?"

"No."

"How did he die?"

"Of an attack of some kind. The doctor who reviewed the report said it was probably a coronary thrombosis."

"Did you make up the report?"

"I wrote it."

"You know what I mean. Was it the truth?"

"It was the truth. It was exactly as it happened."

Slidell turned to Flowers. "Anything yet?"

Flowers shook his head. "No change at all."

"All right, Rogers. You read the letter Reagan wrote to Paula Stafford. He said he had twenty-three thousand dollars with him, and that he was going to ask you to put him ashore somewhere. Nineteen thousand dollars of that money is missing. Keefer didn't have it, and it's not on your boat. If Reagan is dead, where is it?"

"I don't know," I said.

"You stole it."

"I've never even seen it."

"Did Reagan ask you to put him ashore?"

"No."

"In four days he didn't even mention it?"

"No."

"Why didn't he?"

"How do I know?" I said.

Flowers held up a hand. "Run through that sequence again. There's something funny here."

I stared at him. One of us must be mad already.

"You're lying, Rogers," Slidell said. "You have to be. Reagan sailed on that boat for the purpose of having you slip him ashore. He even told Paula Stafford that. You read the letter."

"Yes."

"And you mean to say he didn't even ask you?"

"He never said anything about it at all."

"Why didn't he?"

"I don't know," I said.

"There it is again," Flowers interrupted. "A definite change in emotional response. I think he does know."

"You killed him, didn't you?" Slidell barked.

"No!" I said.

Then I was standing at the rail again on that Sunday afternoon watching the shrouded body fade into the depths below me, and the strange feeling of dread began to come back. I looked at the machine. The styli jerked erratically, making frenzied swings across the paper.

Slidell shoved his face close to mine. *"You and Keefer killed him!"*

"No!" I shouted.

Flowers nodded. "He's lying."

My hands were tightly clenched. I closed my eyes and tried to find the answer in the dark confusion of my thoughts. It was there somewhere, just beyond my reach. In God's name, what was it? The water closed over him and a few bubbles drifted upward with the release of air trapped within the shroud, and he began to fall, sliding deeper and fading from view, and I began to be afraid of something I couldn't even name, and I wanted to bring him back. I heard Patricia Reagan cry out. A hand caught the front of my shirt and I was half lifted from the chair, and Bonner was shouting in my face. I lost it completely then; everything was gone. Slidell's voice cut through the uproar like a knife, and Bonner dropped me, and the room was silent.

"When did you kill him?" Slidell barked.

"I didn't!"

He sighed. "All right. Begin with the first day."

We ran out of the harbor on the auxiliary, between the big stone breakwaters where the surf was booming. Baxter took the wheel while Keefer and I got sail on her. It was past midmorning now and the Trade was picking up, a spanking full-sail breeze out of the northeast with a moderate sea in which she pitched a little and shipped a few dollops of spray that spatted against the canvas and wet the cushions of the cockpit. She was close-hauled on the starboard tack as we began to beat our way offshore.

"How does she handle?" I asked Baxter.

He was bareheaded and shirtless, as we all were, and his eyes were happier than they had been. "Very nicely," he said. "Takes just a little weather helm."

I peered into the binnacle. "Any chance of laying the course?"

He let her come up a little, and slides began to rattle along the luff of the mains'l. The course was still half a point to windward. "It may haul a little more to the easterly as we get offshore," he said.

I took her for a few minutes to see how she felt, and called to Blackie. "If you want to learn to be a helmsman, here's a good time to start."

He grinned cockily, and took the wheel. "This bedpan? I could steer it with a canoe paddle. What's the course?"

"Full-and-by," I told him.

"What's that?"

"It's a term seamen use," I said. "Mr. Baxter'll explain it to you while I make some coffee."

I made sandwiches at noon and took the helm. The breeze freshened and hauled almost a point to the eastward. Baxter relieved me at four with the mountains of Panama growing hazier and beginning to slide into the sea astern. She was heeled over sharply with all sail set, lifting to the sea with a long, easy corkscrew motion as water hissed and gurgled along the lee rail with that satisfying sound that meant she was correctly trimmed and happy and running down the miles. Spray flew aft and felt cool against our faces. When he took the wheel I looked aloft again and then eyed the main sheet with speculation. He smiled, and shook his head, and I agreed with him. You couldn't improve on it.

"What's her waterline length?" he asked.

"Thirty-four," I said.

There is a formula for calculating the absolute maximum speed of a displacement hull, regardless of the type or amount of power applied. It's a function of the trochoidal wave system set up by the boat and is 1.34 times the square root of the waterline length. I could see Baxter working this out now.

"On paper," I said, "she should do a little better than seven and a half knots."

He nodded. "I'd say she was logging close to six."

As I went below to start supper I saw him turn once and look astern at the fading coastline of Panama. When he swung back to face the binnacle, there was an expression of relief or satisfaction in the normally grave brown eyes.

The breeze went down a little with the sun, but she still sang her way along. Keefer took the eight-to-twelve watch and I slept for a few hours. When I came on deck at midnight there was only a light breeze and the sea was going down. . . .

"What the hell is this?" Bonner demanded. He came over in front of us. "Are we going to sail that lousy boat up from Panama mile by mile?"

"Foot by foot, if we have to," Slidell said crisply, "till we find out what happened."

"You'll never do it this way. The machine's no good. He fooled it the first time."

Flowers stared at him with frigid dislike. "Nobody beats this machine. When he starts to lie, it'll tell us."

"Yeah. Sure. Like it did when he said Baxter died of a heart attack."

"Shut up!" Slidell snapped. "Get back out of the way. Take the girl to the kitchen and tell her to make some coffee. And keep your hands off her."

"Why?"

"It would be obvious to anybody but an idiot. I don't want her screaming and upsetting Rogers' emotional response."

We're all crazy, I thought. Maybe everybody who had any contact with Baxter eventually went mad. No, not Baxter. His name was Reagan. I was sitting here hooked up to a shiny electronic gadget like a cow to a milking machine while an acidulous gnome with popeyes extracted the truth from me—truth that I apparently no longer even knew myself. I hadn't killed Reagan. Even if I were mad now, I hadn't been then. Every detail of the trip was clear in my mind. But how could it be? The machine said I was trying to hide something. What? And when had it happened? I put my hands up to my face, and it hurt everywhere I touched it. My eyes were swollen almost shut. I was dead tired. I looked at my watch, and saw it was nearly two p.m. Then it occurred to me that if they had arrived five minutes later I would already have called the FBI. That was nice to think about now.

Bonner jerked his head, and Patricia Reagan arose from the couch and followed him into the kitchen like a sleep-walker, or some long-legged mechanical toy.

"You still have plenty of paper?" Slidell asked Flowers. The latter nodded.

"All right, Rogers," Slidell said. He sat down again, facing me. "Reagan was still alive the morning of the second day—"

"He was alive until after three-thirty p.m., of the fourth day."

He cut me off. "Stop interrupting. He was alive the morning of the second day, and he still hadn't said anything about putting him ashore?"

"Not a word," I said.

He nodded to Flowers to start the paper again. "Go on."

We went on. The room was silent except for the sound of my voice and the faint humming of the air-conditioner. Graph paper crawled slowly across the face of the instrument from one roll to another while the styli kept up their jagged but unvarying scrawls.

Dawn came with light airs and a gently heaving sea, and we were alone with no land visible anywhere. As soon as I could see the horizon, Baxter relieved me so I could take a series of star sights. I worked them out under the hooded light of the chart table while Keefer snored gently in the bunk just forward of me. Two of them appeared to be good. We were eighty-four miles from Cristobal, and had averaged a little better than four and a half knots. We'd made slightly more leeway than I'd expected, however, and I corrected the course.

At seven I called Keefer and began frying eggs and bacon. When I was getting them out of the refrigerator, I noticed it was scarcely more than cool inside and apparently hadn't been running the way it should. After breakfast I checked the batteries of the lighting system, added some distilled water, and ran the generator for a while. We were shaking down to the routine of sea watches now, and Baxter and I were able to get a couple of hours' sleep while Keefer took the morning watch from eight to twelve. He called me at eleven-thirty.

I got a good fix at noon that put us a little over a hundred miles out from Cristobal. Baxter took the wheel while I worked it out, and Keefer made a platter of thick sandwiches with canned corned beef and slices of onion. I ate mine at the wheel after I took over for the twelve-to-four trick. I threw the empty milk carton overboard, watched it fall astern as I tried to estimate our speed, and lighted a cigarette. I was content; this was the way to live.

It was a magnificent day. The wind had freshened a little since early morning and was a moderate easterly breeze now, directly abeam as she ran lightfooted across the miles on the long reach to the northward, heeled down with water creaming along the rail. The sun shone hotly, drying the spray on my face and arms, and sparkling on the face of the sea as the long rollers advanced, lifted us, and went on. I started the main sheet a little, decided it had been right before, and trimmed it again. Baxter came on deck just as I finished. He smiled. "No good sailor is ever satisfied, I suppose."

I grinned. "I expect not. But I thought you'd turned in. Couldn't you sleep?"

"A day like this is too beautiful to waste," he replied. "And I thought I'd get a little sun."

He was wearing a white bathrobe with his cigarettes and lighter in one of the pockets. He lighted a cigarette, slipped off the robe, rolled it into a pillow, and stretched out in the sun along the cushions in the starboard side of the cockpit, wearing only a pair of boxer shorts. He lay feet forward, with his head about even with the wheel. He closed his eyes.

"I was just looking at the chart," he said. "If we keep on logging four to five knots we should be up in the Yucatán Channel by Sunday."

"There's a chance," I said idly. Sunday or Monday, it didn't really matter. I was in no hurry. You trimmed and started the sheets and steered and kept one eye forever on the wind as if that last fraction of a knot were a matter of life or death, but it had nothing to do with saving time. It was simply a matter of craftsmanship, of sailing a boat rather than merely riding on it.

He was silent for a few minutes. Then he asked, "What kind of boat is the *Orion?*"

"Fifty-foot schooner. Gaff-rigged on the fore and jib-headed on the main, and carries a fore-tops'l, stays'l, and working jib. She accommodates a party of six besides the two of us in the crew."

"Is she very old?"

"Yes. Over twenty years now. But sound."

"Upkeep gets to be a problem, though," he said thoughtfully. "I mean, as they get progressively older. What is your basic charter price?"

"Five hundred a week, plus expenses."

"I see," he said. "It seems to me, though, you could do better with something a little larger. Say a good shallow-draft ketch or yawl, about sixty feet. With the right interior layout, it would probably handle more people, so you could raise your charter price. Wouldn't take any larger crew, and if it were still fairly new your maintenance costs might be less."

"Yes, I know," I said. "I've been on the lookout for something like that for a long time, but I've never been able to swing it. It'd take fifteen thousand to twenty thousand more than I could get for the *Orion*."

"Yes," he agreed, "it would be pretty expensive."

We fell silent. He sat up to get another cigarette from the pocket of his robe. I thought I heard him say something, and glanced up from the compass card. "I beg your pardon?"

He made no reply. He was turned slightly away from me, facing forward, so I saw only the back of his head. He had the lighter in his hand as if he'd started to light the cigarette and then had forgotten it. He tilted his head back, stretching his neck, and put a hand up to the base of his throat.

"Something wrong?" I asked.

It was almost a full minute before he answered. I glanced at the compass card, and brought the wheel up a spoke. "Oh," he said quietly. "No. Just a touch of indigestion."

I grinned. "That's not much of a recommendation for Blackie's sandwiches." Then I thought uneasily of the refrigerator; food poisoning could be a very dangerous thing at sea. But the corned beef was canned; it couldn't have been spoiled. And the milk had tasted all right.

"It was the onions," he said. "I should never eat them."

"There's some bicarbonate in one of the lockers above the sink," I told him.

"I have something here," he said. He carefully dropped the lighter back in the pocket of his robe and took out a small bottle of pills. He shook one out and put it in his mouth.

"Hold the wheel," I said, "and I'll get you some water."

"Thanks," he said. "I don't need it."

He lay back with his head pillowed on the robe and his eyes closed. Once or twice he shifted a little and drew his knees up as if he were uncomfortable, but he said nothing further about it except to reply with a brief "Yes" when I asked if he felt better. After a while he groped for the bottle and took another of the pills, and then lay quietly for a half hour, apparently asleep. His face and body were shiny with sweat as the sun beat down on him, and I began to be afraid he'd get a bad burn. I touched him on the shoulder to wake him up.

"Don't overdo it the first day," I said.

He wasn't asleep, however. "Yes, I expect you're right,"

he replied. "I think I'll turn in." He got up a little un-steadily and made his way down the companion ladder. After he was gone I noticed he'd forgotten to take the robe. I rolled it tightly and wedged it in back of a cushion so it wouldn't blow overboard.

A school of porpoises picked us up and escorted us for a while, leaping playfully about the bow. I watched them, en-joying their company as I always did at sea. In about a half hour Keefer came up from below carrying a mug of coffee. He sat down in the cockpit.

"You want a cup?" he asked.

I looked at my watch. It was three now. "No, thanks. I'll get one after Baxter takes over."

"We ought to have our tails kicked," he said, "for not thinking to buy a fish line. At this speed we could pick up a dolphin or barracuda."

"I intended to," I said, "but forgot it."

We talked for a while about trolling. Nowadays, when practically all ships made sixteen knots or better, it was out of the question, but when he'd first started going to sea just before the Second World War he'd been on a few of the old eight- and ten-knot tankers on the coastwise run from Texas to the East Coast, and sometimes in the Stream they'd rig a trolling line of heavy sashcord with an inner tube for a snubber. Usually the fish tore off or straightened the hook, but occasionally they'd manage to land one.

He stood up and stretched. "Well, I think I'll flake out again."

He started below. Just as his shoulders were disappearing down the companion hatch my eyes fell on Baxter's robe, which was getting wet with spray. "Here," I called out, "take this down, will you?"

I rolled it tightly and tossed it. The distance wasn't more than eight feet, but just before it reached his outstretched hand a freakish gust of wind found an opening and it ballooned suddenly and was snatched to leeward. I sprang from the wheel and lunged for it, but it sailed under the mizzen boom, landed in the water a good ten feet away, and began to fall astern. I looked out at it and cursed myself for an idiot.

"Stand by the backstay!" I called out to Keefer. "We'll go about and pick it up."

Then I remembered we hadn't tacked once since our departure from Cristobal. By the time I'd explained to him about casting off the weather backstay and setting it up on the other side as we came about, the robe was a good hundred and fifty yards astern. "Hard a-lee!" I shouted, and put the helm down. We came up into the wind with the sails slatting. I cast off the port jib sheet and trimmed the starboard one. They ran aft through fairleads to winches at the forward end of the cockpit. Blackie set up the runner. We filled away, and I put the wheel hard over to bring her back across our wake. I steadied her up just to leeward of it.

"Can you see it?" I yelled to Keefer.

"Dead ahead, about a hundred yards," he called back. "But it's beginning to sink."

"Take the wheel!" I ordered. I slid a boathook from under its lashing atop the doghouse and ran forward. I could see it. It was about fifty yards ahead, but only a small part of it still showed above the surface. "Left just a little!" I sang out. "Steady, right there!"

It disappeared. I marked the spot, and as we bore down on it I knelt at the rail just forward of the mainmast and peered down with the boathook poised. We came over the spot. Then I saw it directly below me, three or four feet under the surface now, a white shape drifting slowly downward through the translucent blue of the water. . . .

"Look!" Flowers cried out.

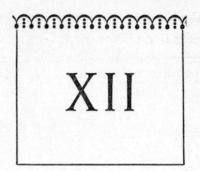

XII

THEY crowded around the table, staring down at the instrument and the sudden, spasmodic jerking of its styli.

I gripped the arms of the chair as it all began falling into place—the nameless fear, and what had actually caused it, and the apparently insignificant thing that had lodged in my subconscious mind on an afternoon sixteen years ago aboard another boat, a chartered sport fisherman off Miami Beach. I *had* killed Baxter. Or at least I was responsible for his death.

Bonner growled, and swung around to grab me by the shirt. "You're lying! So now let's hear what really happened—"

I tried to swing at his face, but Slidell grabbed my arm before I could pull the instrument off the table by its connecting wires. "Shut up!" I roared. "Get off my back, you stupid ape! I'm trying to understand it myself!"

Slidell waved him off. "Get away!" Bonner stepped back, and Slidell spoke to me. "You didn't get the bathrobe?"

"No," I said. All the rage went out of me suddenly, and I leaned back in the chair with my eyes closed. "I touched it with the end of the boathook, but I couldn't get hold of it."

That was what I'd seen, but hadn't wanted to see, the afternoon we buried him. It wasn't his body, sewn in white Orlon, that was fading away below me, disappearing forever into two miles of water; it was that damned white bathrobe. And all the time I was trying to bury it in my subconscious, the other thing—already buried there—was trying to dig it up.

"And they were the only ones he had?" Slidell asked.

"I guess so," I said dully. I could hear Patricia Reagan crying softly over to my left.

Bonner's rasping voice cut in. "What the hell are you talking about?"

Slidell paid no attention. Or maybe he gestured for him to shut up. My eyes were still closed.

"And he still didn't tell you what they were?" Slidell went on. "You didn't realize it until he had the second one, the one that killed him—"

"Look!" I cried out angrily. "I didn't even realize it then! Why should I? He said it was indigestion, and he took a pill for it, and then he took another one, and he lay there resting and getting a suntan for about a half hour and then went below and turned in. He didn't groan, or cry out. It wasn't anything like the other one; the pain probably wasn't anywhere near as bad, or he wouldn't have been able to cover it up that way.

"I had no reason to connect the two. I understand now why he didn't say anything about it, even when I told him about the bathrobe. He knew I'd take him back to Panama, and he'd rather risk another ten days at sea without the medicine than do that. But why would I have any reason to suspect it? All I knew about him was what he'd told me. His name was Wendell Baxter, and he got indigestion when he ate onions."

No, I thought; that wasn't completely true. Then, before I could correct myself, Flowers' voice broke in. "Wait a minute—"

He'd never even looked up, I thought; people as such didn't really exist for him; they were just some sort of stimulating devices or power supplies he hooked onto his damned machine so he could sit there and stare enraptured into its changing expressions. Maybe this was what they meant about the one-sided development of genius.

"All right," I said. "I'm lying. Or I was. I was lying to myself. There was a reason I should have known it was a heart attack, but I didn't understand what it was until today, when I thought about the one my uncle had."

"What was that?" Slidell asked.

"He didn't swallow those pills," I said.

"Why?" Bonner asked. "What's that got to do with it?"

"They were nitroglycerin," Slidell told him impatiently. I straightened up in the chair and groped mechanically for a cigarette.

"I think it must have stuck in my mind all those years,"

I went on. "I mean, it was the first time I'd ever heard of pills you took but didn't swallow. You dissolved them under your tongue. Reagan was doing the same thing, but it didn't quite click until just now. I merely thought he was swallowing them without water."

Slidell sat down again, lighted a cigarette, and regarded me with a bleak smile. "It's regrettable your medical knowledge isn't as comprehensive as that stupid conscience of yours and its defense mechanisms, Rogers. It would have saved us a lot of time."

I frowned. "What do you mean?"

"That it probably wouldn't have made the slightest difference if he'd had a tubful of those nitroglycerin pills. They're a treatment for angina, which is essentially just the warning. The danger signal. Reagan, from your report, was killed by a really massive coronary, and you could just as well have given him aspirin or a Bromo-Seltzer."

"How do you know so much about it?" I asked.

"I went to a doctor and asked," he said. "When you're dealing with sums in the order of a half million dollars you cover all bases. But never mind. Let's get on with it."

I wondered what he hoped to find out now, but I didn't say it aloud. With Reagan admittedly dead and lying on the bottom of the Caribbean with his secret the show was over, but as long as he refused to accept it and kept me tied to this machine answering questions Patricia Reagan and I would stay alive. When he gave up, Bonner would get rid of us. It was as simple as that.

"We can assume," he went on, "that we know now why Reagan didn't ask you to put him ashore. That first heart attack—and losing his medicine—scared him off. There's no doubt he'd already been suffering from angina, or he wouldn't have had the nitroglycerin, but this was more than that—or he thought it was, which amounts to the same thing. Of course, he still might die before he reached Southport, but even at that he'd have a better chance staying with the boat than he would landing on a deserted stretch of beach and having to fight his way through a bunch of jungle alone. So he played the percentages."

"Yes," I said. That seemed more or less obvious now.

"What was he wearing when he died?"

"Dungarees," I said, "and a pair of sneakers."

"If he'd had a money belt around him, you would have seen it?"

"Yes. But he didn't have one."

Flowers and Bonner were silently watching the machine. I turned and shot a glance at Patricia Reagan. Her face was pale, but she didn't avoid my eyes now. That was something, anyway. Maybe she didn't blame me for his death.

"Did you put any more clothes on him when you buried him?"

"No," I said.

"And everything he owned was turned over to the US marshal?"

"That's right."

He exhaled smoke and stared up at the ceiling. "Now I think we're getting somewhere, wouldn't you say? Somewhere around nineteen thousand dollars of that money is still missing. It didn't go ashore with his things, it wasn't buried with him, Keefer didn't have it, you haven't got it, and I don't think there's a chance it's on your boat. What does that leave?"

"Nothing," I said. "Unless he just didn't have it with him."

He smiled coldly. "But I think he did."

I began to get it then. You had to remember two things. The first was that he wasn't even remotely interested in $19,000 worth of chicken-feed; from his point of view the fact that it was missing was the only good news he had left. And the other thing you had to keep in mind was that Reagan had been warned. He knew there was at least a chance he wouldn't reach the States alive.

Excitement quickened along my nerves. All the pieces were beginning to make sense now, and I should know where that money was. And not only the money. The same thing he was looking for—a letter. I could have done it long ago, I thought, if I hadn't subconsciously tried to reject the idea that I was to blame for Reagan's death.

"Here's something," Flowers called out softly.

I glanced up then, and finally realized the real beauty of the trap they had me in. Even thinking of the answer would get me killed. Bonner's hard eyes were on my face, and Slidell was watching me with the poised deadliness of a stalking cat.

"Have you thought of something?" he asked.

The telephone rang.

The unexpected sound of it seemed to explode in the silence, and everybody turned to look at it except Slidell. He stood up and nodded curtly to Patricia Reagan. "Answer it, and get rid of whoever it is. If it's somebody looking for

Rogers, he left. You don't know where he went. Under-stand?"

She faced him for a moment, and then nodded, and crossed unsteadily to the desk. He was beside her as she picked up the receiver, and motioned for her to tilt it so he could hear too. Bonner turned and watched me. "Hello," she said. Then, "Yes. That's right."

There was a longer pause. Then she said, "Yes. He was here. But he left. . . . No, he didn't say. . . ."

So it was Bill. She was listening. She looked helplessly at Slidell. He pulled the receiver down, put his hand over it, and said, "Tell him no. It couldn't have been. And hang up."

She repeated it. "You're welcome," she said, and replaced the instrument.

What would he do now? There was no doubt as to what he'd asked. And I'd told him if the Reagan lead proved a dead end I was going to call the FBI. As a reporter he could conceivably find out whether I had or not. How much time would go by before he decided something was wrong? It was only a very slight one, and there was no way he could have known, but Slidell had finally made a mistake.

He motioned for her to go back, and picked up the phone himself. "Southport, Texas," he said. "The Randall Hotel, and I want to speak to Mr. Shaw."

He held on. Patricia sat down on the couch, and when I turned toward her she made a helpless, almost apologetic sort of gesture, and tried to smile. I nodded and tried it my-self, but it wasn't much more successful.

"Hello?" Slidell said. "Yes. Some progress here. We ran

into an old friend, and we're having quite a discussion. Anything new there? . . . I see. . . . But they still haven't been able to talk to her? . . . Good. . . . What about the other one? . . . That's fine. . . . Sounds just about right. Well, stand by. I'll call you when we get something." He hung up.

There were only parts of it I understood. One man was still in Southport, covering that end of it. Paula Stafford was alive, but the police hadn't been able to question her yet, as far as he knew. But I couldn't guess what he meant by the "other one."

He came back and sat down. I wondered what Bill would do, and how much longer we had.

"Let's consider what Reagan would do," he said. "He knew he could die before he reached the States. You would turn his suitcase over to the US marshal or the police, and the money would be discovered. At first glance, that would seem to be no great hardship, since he wouldn't need it any longer, but it's not quite that simple. I've made a rather thorough study of Reagan—anybody who steals a half million dollars from me is almost certain to arouse my interest —and he was quite a complex man. He was a thief, but an uncomfortable thief, if you follow me. It was gambling that always got him into trouble. But all that's beside the point. What I'm getting at is that he loved his daughter very much. He'd made a mess of his life—that is, from his viewpoint— and while he was willing to take the consequences himself, he'd do almost anything to keep from hurting her again."

Patricia made a little outcry. Slidell glanced at her indifferently and went on.

"I'm fairly certain the real reason, or at least one reason, he agreed to go along with us is that he'd been dipping into the till at the Drovers National, as he had at the other bank, and he saw a way to put the money back before they caught up with him. But there was risk in this too, so he decided to take it all and fade.

"At any rate, if you're still following me, he was dead, buried, and honest, as far as his daughter was concerned. But if all that money came to light there'd be an investigation, eventually they'd find out who he really was, and she'd have to bury him all over again, this time as one of the most publicized thieves since Dillinger.

"So he had to do something with it? But what? Throw it overboard? That might seem just a little extreme later on when he arrived in Southport still in good health. Hide it somewhere on the boat? That would be more like it, because then if he arrived all right he merely pulled it out of the hiding place and went on his way. But there are two difficulties; it'd be pretty hard, if not downright impossible, to hide anything permanently on a forty-foot boat, to begin with, and then there was Paula Stafford. She knew he had it, of course, so when it turned up missing she might come out of hiding and jump you about it, which could lead to an investigation, the very thing he was trying to avoid. And there's no doubt he would much rather she had it anyway. *Along with the rest of it.* So the chances are he'd try to arrange for her to get it, in case he died, without anyone's ever knowing he had it aboard. But how? And what went wrong?"

He was approaching it from a different direction, but he was leading me toward it as inevitably as I'd been headed for it myself. I wondered how near we would get before the machine betrayed me, or before the conscious effort of my holding back was written there in its jagged scrawls for Flowers to see. The things it measured were outside voluntary control.

His eyes shifted from the machine to my face like those of a big cat, just waiting. "We don't know how he tried to do it. But what went wrong, obviously, was Keefer. When he had the big one, how long was it from the time it struck until he died?"

"I guessed it at about twenty minutes," I said. "Naturally, I wasn't watching a clock. And it's not an easy thing to tell, anyway, in spite of the offhand way they do it on television. He could have been dead five or ten minutes before we were sure." Add all the details possible, I thought, as long as they're true and don't really matter.

"Thank you, Doctor," he said, with a bleak smile. "Approximately how long was he conscious?"

"Just the first few minutes. Five at the most."

"He didn't say anything?"

"No." Nothing coherent, I started to add, but thought better of it. She was having a bad enough time of it as it was without being told the kind of sounds he made.

"Was Keefer alone with him at any time?"

"No," I said.

"So he was the one who went to look in the suitcase for medicine?"

"Yes."

Flowers was watching the scrawls with rapt attention, but he had said nothing yet. As long as I concentrated on one question at a time I was all right. But each one was a step, leading up to where the noose was waiting.

"When did you inventory his things?"

"The next morning."

"And at least half of that time you would have been on deck, at the wheel, while he was below alone?"

"If you mean could he have gone through Reagan's suit-case," I said coldly, "of course he could. And he probably did, since he had four thousand dollars when we arrived in Southport. But he couldn't have carried twenty-three thou-sand ashore with him unless it was in five hundred- or thousand-dollar bills. He didn't have it, anyway, or the po-lice would have found it."

"I know that," he broke in. "But let's plug all the holes as we go. You docked in Southport Monday afternoon, the sixteenth. Was that at the boatyard?"

"No," I said. "We didn't go alongside a pier at all that day. We anchored at the City Yacht Basin."

"Did you go ashore?"

"I didn't. Keefer did. He put the bite on me for another twenty-dollar advance and went uptown."

"Then he wasn't entirely stupid. You knew he was broke, so he had sense enough to ask you for money. Could he have been carrying any of it then?"

"Not much," I said. "I was below when he washed up and dressed, so he didn't have it tied around his body any-where. I saw his wallet when he put the twenty in it. It was empty. He couldn't have carried much just in his pockets."

"You didn't leave the boat at all?"

"Only when I rowed him over to the pier in the dinghy.

I went over to the phone in the yacht club and called the estimators in a couple of boatyards to have them come look the job over."

"What time did Keefer come back?"

"The next morning, around eight. About half drunk."

"He must have had some of the money, then, unless he set a world's record for milking a twenty. What about that morning?"

"He shaved and had a cup of coffee, and we went up to the US marshal's office. He couldn't have picked up anything aboard the boat because it was only about ten minutes and I was right there all the time. We spent the morning with the marshal and the Coast Guard, and went back to the Yacht Basin about two-thirty p.m. I paid him the rest of his money, he rolled up the two pairs of dungarees, the only clothes he had to carry, and I rowed him over to the pier. He couldn't have put anything in the dungarees. I wasn't watching him deliberately, of course; I just happened to be standing there talking to him. He rode off with the truck from Harley's boatyard. They'd brought me some gasoline so I could get over to the yard; the tanks were dry because we'd used it all trying to get back to Cristobal when we were becalmed. The police say he definitely had three to four thousand with him a half hour later when he checked in at the hotel, so he must have had it in his wallet."

"You moved the boat to Harley's boatyard that afternoon, then? Did you go ashore that night?"

"No."

"Wednesday night?"

"No," I said. "Both nights I went up to that Domino

place for a bite to eat and was gone a half hour or forty-five minutes at the most, and that was before dark. I had too much work to do for any night life."

"You didn't see Keefer at all during that time?"

"No," I said.

"But you did go ashore Thursday night, and didn't get back till twelve. Keefer could have gone aboard then."

"Past the watchman at the gate?" I said, wondering if I would get by with it. "The cabin of the boat was locked, anyway."

"With a padlock anybody could open with one rap of a stale doughnut."

"Not without making enough noise to be heard out at the gate," I said. "That's the reason your man used bolt-cutters on the hasp."

We were skirting dangerously close now, and I had to decide in the next minute or so what I was going to do. Sweat it out, and hope they would hold off until that man in Southport could go check? It would be another seven or eight hours before he'd be able to, because he'd have to wait at least until after it was dark, and even as isolated as this place was they couldn't hang around forever. And as he had said, we were closing the holes as we went; when we got to the last one, what was left?

"How many keys were there to that padlock?" he asked.

"Only one," I said, "as far as I know."

"But there could have been another one around. Padlocks always come with two, and the lock must have been aboard when you bought the boat. Where was the key kept when you were at sea?"

"In a drawer in the galley. Along with the lock."

"So if Keefer wanted to be sure of getting back in later on, he had ten days to practice picking that lock. Or to make an impression of the key so he could have a duplicate made. It wouldn't take much more than a hundred-and-forty IQ to work that out, would it?"

"No," I said.

"All right. He had the rest of that money hidden somewhere in the cabin so he could pick it up when you weren't around. You and the yard people were working on the boat during the day, and you didn't go ashore at night, so he was out of luck for the next two days. Then Thursday night you went uptown to a movie. You'd hardly got out of sight when he showed up at the gate and tried to con the watchman into letting him go aboard. The watchman wouldn't let him in. So he did the same thing we did, picked up a skiff over at that next dock where all the fishing boats were, and went in the back way."

"It's possible," I said. "But you're only guessing."

"No. Shaw talked to that girl he was with in the Domino. She said Keefer was supposed to pick her up at eight-thirty. He called and said he might be a little late, and it was almost ten when he finally showed. Now guess where he'd been."

"Okay," I said. "But if he came aboard and got it, what became of it? He picked the girl up at ten, he was with her until I ran into them a little before midnight, and you know what happened to him after that."

He smiled coldly. "Those were the last two holes. He didn't give it to the girl, and we know he didn't throw it out of the car when Bonner and Shaw ran him to the curb about twenty minutes later and picked him up to ask him about Reagan. Therefore, he never did get it. When he got aboard, it was gone."

"Gone?" I asked. "You mean you think I found it?"

He shook his head. "What equipment was removed from that boat for repairs?"

"The refrigerator," I said, and dived for him.

He'd been watching Flowers, and was already reaching for the gun.

XIII

I was on him before it came clear. His chair went over backward under the two of us. I felt the tug of the wires connecting me to the lie-detector as I came out to the end of their slack, and I heard it crash to the floor behind us, bringing the table with it. Flowers gave a shrill cry, whether of outrage or terror I couldn't tell, and ran past us toward the door.

Slidell and I were in a hopeless tangle, still propped against the upended chair as we fought for the gun. He had it out of his pocket now. I grabbed it by the cylinder and barrel with my left hand, forcing it away from me, and tried to hit him with a right, but the wire connected to my arm was fouled somewhere in the mess now and it brought me up short. Then Bonner was standing over us. The blackjack sliced down, missing my head and cutting across my shoulder. I heaved, rolling Slidell over on top of me. For an instant I could see the couch where she had been sitting. She was gone. Thank God, she'd run the second I'd lunged at him. If she had enough lead, she might get away.

We heaved over once more, with Bonner cutting at me again with the blackjack, and then I saw her. She hadn't run. She'd just reached the telephone and was lifting it off the cradle and starting to dial. I heard Bonner snarl. Slidell and I rolled again, and I couldn't see her, but then I heard the sound of the blow and her cry as she fell.

My arm was free now. I hit Slidell in the face. He grunted, but still held onto the gun, trying to swing it around to get the muzzle against me. I hit him again. His hold on it was weakening. I beat at him with rage and frustration. Wouldn't he ever let go? Then Bonner was leaning over us, taking the gun out of both our hands. Beyond him I saw Patricia Reagan getting up from the floor, beside the telephone where Bonner had tossed it after he'd pulled the cord out of the wall. She grasped the corner of the desk and reached for something on it. I wanted to scream for her to get out. If she could only understand that if one of us got away they might give it up and run . . .

Just as he got the gun away from us she came up behind him swinging the 35-mm camera by its strap. It caught him just above the ear and he grunted and fell to his knees. The gun slid out of his fingers. I grabbed it, and then Slidell had it by the muzzle.

"Run!" I yelled at her. "Get away! The police!"

She understood then. She wheeled and ran out the front door.

Slidell raged at Bonner. "Go get her!"

Bonner shook his head like a fighter who's just taken a nine count, pushed to his feet, and looked about the room.

He rubbed a hand across his face and ran toward the back door.

"The front!" Slidell screamed. He tore at the gun and tried to knee me in the groin. I slid sidewise away from him, avoiding it, and hit him high on the side of the face. Jagged slivers of pain went up my arm. Bonner turned and ran out the front door. I jerked on the gun, and this time I broke Slidell's grip. I rolled away from him and climbed to my feet. My knees trembled. I was sobbing for breath, and the whole room was turning. When the front door came by I lunged for it. But the wreckage of the lie-detector was still fast to my right arm; it spun me around and threw me off balance just as Slidell scrambled up and hit me at the waist with a hard-driving tackle. We fell across the edge of the table the instrument had been on. Pain sliced its way through my left side and made me cry out, and I heard the ribs go like the snapping of half-green sticks. The table gave way under us, and when we landed the gun was under me. I pulled it free, shifted it from my left hand to the right, and hit him across the left temple with it just as he was pushing up to his knees. He grunted and fell face down in what was left of the table.

I made it to my feet, and this time I remembered Flowers' beloved machine. I tried to unwrap the pressure cuff from around my arm, but my fingers were trembling and I couldn't half see, so I stepped on the machine and pulled upward against the wire. It broke. The one to the tube around my chest had already parted. I ran to the front door. A steel trap of pain clamped shut around my left side. I bent over with my hand against it and kept going.

The sunlight was blinding after the dimness inside. I saw

Bonner. He was a good hundred yards away, near the mailbox, running very fast for a man with his squat, heavy build. I started after him. She wasn't in sight from here, but he turned left, toward the highway, when he reached the road.

My torso felt as if it had been emptied and then stuffed with broken glass or eggshells. Every breath was agony, and I ran awkwardly, with a feeling that I had been cut in two and the upper half of my body was merely riding, none too well balanced, on the lower. Then I saw her. She was running along the marl road less than fifty yards ahead of him. He was gaining rapidly. Just as I came out onto the road she looked back and saw him. She plunged off to the right, running through the palmetto and stunted pine to try to hide. I would never get there in time. I raised the gun and shot, knowing I couldn't hit him at that distance but hoping the sound would stop him. He paid no attention. Then he was off the road, closing in on her.

I plunged after him. For a moment I lost them and was terrified. It wouldn't take him more than a minute to kill her. Why didn't she scream? I tore through a screen of brush then and saw them in an open area surrounding a small salt pond. She ran out into it, trying to get across. The water was a little more than knee-deep. She stumbled and fell, and he was on her before she could get up. He bent down, caught her by the hair, and held her head under.

I tried to yell, but the last of my breath was gone. My foot caught in a mangrove root and I fell into the mud just at the edge of the water. He heard me. He straightened, and looked around. She threshed feebly, tried to get up, but fell back with her face under water.

"Pick—pick—" I gasped. "Lift her—"

He faced me contemptuously. "You come and get her."

I cocked the gun, rested it across my left forearm, and shot him through the chest. His knees folded and he collapsed face down. When I got to her the water around him was growing red, and he jerked convulsively and drew his legs up and kicked, driving his head against my legs as I put my arms around her shoulders and lifted. I got her out somehow, up beyond the slimy mud, and when she choked a few times and began to breathe I walked another few steps and fell on my knees and was sick.

After a while we started out to the highway and a phone. When the police got back to the house they picked up Slidell over in the pines trying to bridge the switch on their rented car. The keys were in Bonner's pocket.

A doctor in Marathon taped my side, and by that time the FBI men were there. They took me to a hospital in Miami for X-rays and more tape and a private room that seemed to be full of people asking questions. They said Patricia Reagan had been examined and found to be all right, and she had gone to a hotel. I finally fell asleep, and when I awoke in the morning with a steel-rigid side and a battered face through which I could see just faintly, there were some more FBI men, and after they were gone Bill came in.

"Brother, what a face," he said. "If that's the only way to become a celebrity, include me out."

Soames, the FBI agent in Southport, had found the letter. It was in the door of the *Topaz'* refrigerator, in the electrical shop at the Harley boatyard, along with a large Manila envelope containing $19,000. It was a thick door, wood on the outside and enameled steel inside, and packed with insulation. Keefer had taken out some screws, pulled away the steel enough to remove some of the insulation, and put in the envelope. That wasn't what caused it to need repairs, of course; the trouble was in the refrigeration unit itself and had begun the first day out of Panama. If Keefer hadn't been an indifferent sailor who never paid any attention to what went on aboard a boat he might have known I'd have it overhauled when we got to the yard.

Reagan had worked it out very cleverly. The letter was in a separate airmail envelope, stamped, addressed to Paula Stafford, but not sealed. The money was in this large Manila deal he'd found on the boat; it had originally held some Hydrographic Office bulletins. But he hadn't merely stuffed the money in, by single bills or bundles; he had packed it in a dozen or more individual letter-sized envelopes and sealed them, so that when the big one was closed it felt like a bunch of letters. It was sealed—or had been until Keefer tore it open.

The letter read:

> YACHT *Topaz*
> AT SEA, JUNE 3RD
>
> *My Darling Paula:*
>   I don't really know how to start this—
>   I write it with a heavy heart, for if you read it at all it will only be because I am dead. The truth is that I have been troubled by angina for some time, and yesterday I suffered what I think was a coronary attack.

And while there is no reason to think I might have
another before we reach port, I felt I should write this
just in case one did cause my death before I had a
chance to say my last good-by to you.

I am afraid this has changed my plans for the future
that I wrote you about, but if I arrive safely in Southport we can discuss new ones when we are together.
I still have all your precious letters that have meant so
much to me. They are in an envelope in my bag, which
will be sent to you in case I have a fatal attack before
we reach port.

My darling, I hope you never receive this letter. But
if you do, remember that I love you and that my last
thoughts were of you.

Forever,
Wendell

"Very neat," Bill said. "This one would have been open
in the suitcase, so you'd read it to find out whom to notify
and where to ship his stuff. And naturally you wouldn't
open a sealed package of old love letters. Inside the sealed
envelope with the money there was another note to her,
this one signed Brian, saying he'd put the other suitcase in
a bonded warehouse of the Rainey Transfer and Storage
Company in New York. Enclosed was the storage receipt
and a letter signed Charles Wayne authorizing the Rainey
people to turn the bag over to her. He told her to get it, but
if Slidell caught up with her to turn it over to him rather
than try to run any longer."

I nodded. It made my face hurt. "Apparently we were
wrong, though, about Keefer's first seeing the money when
he went to search the bag for medicine. The big envelope

was already sealed then. So he must have seen Reagan when he was fixing it up."

Bill grinned. "Well, it's lucky old Nosy Keefer smelled even more and bigger money in the letter and decided to hang onto it too. If he'd thrown it overboard, you might have been an old man before it was settled to everybody's satisfaction that Reagan did have a bad heart. Think of trying to run down the doctor who wrote the prescription for those nitro pills, with the places Reagan had been and the names he'd used the past two months."

"Lay off," I said. "It still scares me. Have they found out yet who Slidell is?"

He lighted a cigarette and gestured toward the paper. "Big-shot hoodlum from Los Angeles. Several arrests for extortion and a couple for murder, but no convictions. The bonds came from three or four big bank robberies in Texas and Oklahoma. They're not sure yet whether Slidell actually took part, or just planned them. Ran with the café-society set quite a bit, or what passes for it in Southern California, and owned a home in Phoenix. Funny part is he came from about the same kind of family background Reagan did, and was well educated, even a couple of years in medical school. Bonner was his bodyguard and hunker and general muscle man. The FBI was able to talk to the Stafford woman last night, and they got the suitcase out of the warehouse in New York, but they're still buttoned up as to how much it was. They're pretty sure she didn't know anything about where it had come from, or that her boy friend's real name was Clifford Reagan. When he closed the book, pal, he closed it."

I looked out the window. "What about Bonner? Nobody's said anything yet."

"Justifiable homicide, what else? They took her statement this morning. Were you supposed to stand there and watch him kill her?"

I didn't say anything. In the movies and on television, I thought, you point the gun and everybody obeys, but maybe they didn't run into Bonners very often. There hadn't been any choice. But it would be a long time before I forgot the horror of that moment when he kicked out with his legs and nudged his head against me in the reddening water. If I ever forgot it.

I was waiting impatiently when Patricia Reagan finally came to see me that afternoon. She'd gone back to close the house and get her things. She was fully recovered, and looked lovely except for a little puffiness on one side of her face. I wanted to pay for the damage to the furnishings and having the phone reinstalled. We argued amicably about it and finally decided we'd share the responsibility. We talked for a while, sticking pretty closely to boats and sailing, the things we both knew and loved, but it trailed off and she left.

She came back again, the following afternoon, and it was the same thing. I was waiting eagerly for her, she seemed prettier each time, and apparently was glad to see me, she smiled, we talked happily about the Bahamas and about her future in photo journalism, and how we'd go out to the Islands where she could shoot some really terrific pictures, and then it began to trail off and we grew polite and formal with each other.

Just before she left, Bill and Lorraine showed up. Bill had already met her, but I introduced her to Lorraine.

After she'd gone, Lorraine looked at me with that old matchmaker's gleam in her eye. "There's a really stunning girl, Rogers, old boy. What's between you two?"

"Her father," I said.

I had a card from her after she'd gone back to Santa Barbara, but I never saw her again.